Praise for Joan Brady's
GOD ON A HARLEY

"*The Bridges of Madison County* meets *The Celestine Prophecy* meets *Self* magazine. . . ."
—*Entertainment Weekly*

"Funny and enjoyable. . . . A whimsical tale of a journey toward spiritual fulfillment."
—*Publishers Weekly*

"A wonderful tale of how God works with [Christine], understanding every one of her heart's desires and knowing her real needs far better than she does."
—Noelle Denke, *The Light Connection*

"A funny and touching look at one woman's spiritual journey."
—*Indianapolis News*

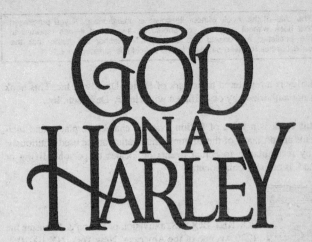

GOD ON A HARLEY

JOAN BRADY

POCKET BOOKS

New York   London   Toronto   Sydney   Tokyo   Singapore

Harley is a registered trademark of Harley-Davidson, Inc. This book is not authorized by or affiliated with Harley-Davidson, Inc.

This book is a work of fiction. Names, characters, places and incidents are products of the author's imagination or are used fictitiously. Any resemblance to actual events or locales or persons, living or dead, is entirely coincidental.

POCKET BOOKS, a division of Simon & Schuster Inc.
1230 Avenue of the Americas, New York, NY 10020

ISBN: 0-671-00278-3

First Pocket Books paperback printing July 1996

10 9 8 7 6 5 4 3

POCKET and colophon are registered trademarks of Simon & Schuster Inc.

Front cover illustration by Ben Perini

Printed in the U.S.A.

To my precious angel, Tommy
and
To Reggie, king of the Jersey shore

Acknowledgments

Grateful acknowledgment is expressed to Denise Stinson, my agent, for turning the key that unlocked a new world for me; to my editor Emily Bestler and to Eric Rayman of Pocket Books for patiently and expertly guiding me through the process; and most especially, to the spiritual force within us all.

I'LL BE THE FIRST TO ADMIT I never understood why they call it The Garden State. I especially didn't understand why, after a seven-year sabbatical on the West Coast, I actually felt happy to be back in New Jersey. After all, everyone pictures New Jersey with the noxious, industrial fumes hovering over the turnpike in Newark rather than the lush, autumn foliage of the Garden State Parkway. Our state is the butt of every joke on the late-night talk shows, and never do they mention what a good sense of humor we have for enduring all the derogatory remarks. They also wrongly assume we Jersey-ites have a collective inferiority complex from living right next door to New York, the city that never sleeps. No matter. We're not the ones who got bombed by terrorists either. Maybe someone finally figured we've had enough hard luck.

Let the critics laugh. We have something New Yorkers will never have, the Jersey shore. Anyone who's spent even one moonlit or sunlit hour here, will tell you how it can stir the latent romance that dwells in even the most cynical New Yorker's soul. Jay Leno and the gang can make all the "Joisey" jokes they want, but that's because they've probably never seen it when the white surf is pounding the salt into the evening air and the moon looks like an orange English muffin popping out of a toaster of clouds.

That's how it looked the first night I drove along Interstate 95 and finally pulled up in front of my new apartment complex only five blocks from the beach. I'd made the arrangements from Los Angeles over the phone and had driven cross-country in only four days. For some reason, I'd felt an urgency to get back to all that was familiar to me, and credit cards and fax machines made that kind of a move incredibly simple. Expensive maybe, but incredibly simple.

In a way, it even felt good to be back in the old familiar corridors of Valley Community Hospital. In spite of dire warnings from West Coast friends who said I'd have a hard time getting a nursing position, thanks to the rampant "downsizing" of hospitals lately, I immediately got a job. Ironically, I was hired back into my old position of three-to-eleven Charge Nurse on the Surgical Trauma Unit. Even though I was suffering from a world-class case of nursing burnout, there was a certain comfort in the familiarity of the well-worn hallways and stairwells that held so much history for me. I felt something like a battle-weary soldier who found himself inexplicably drawn to the trenches and foxholes where, at one time, he had fought for his very life.

During the fifteen years of my nursing career, I'd worked in hospitals all across the country in a never-ending search for a nursing job that didn't deplete my very soul. I never found one I could bear to make permanent, and now it seemed, I had come full circle. I was back where it all had started, and the memories, most of them unpleasant, intruded like uninvited guests. I must have walked at least a million miles through these old, paint-chipped corridors and climbed the back stairs enough times to circle the moon. The gray, cement-block walls were the same ones I'd leaned against many a night, so bone-tired that my back felt like a pack mule and my feet felt like two dead clumps of flesh hanging off my ankles.

But there had been an up side too. I'd managed to fall in love a time or two in this old, crumbling House of Wretchedness. Oh, those were the days. Stolen kisses in empty elevators. Steamy moments in deserted stairwells. Faces obscured by surgical masks with eyes that said things that lips never could. Love among the ruins. Irrepressible love that sprang up among the drama and agony of an inner city hospital, like blades of grass that manage to push their way through and thrive in the cracks of a concrete sidewalk. I was young and romantic then. I had dreams of falling madly in love and getting married. Dreams that died a painful and lingering death.

Now here I was again, back in the ring for round two, but not at all prepared for it. I comforted myself with the fact that at least I was older and hopefully wiser now. I would never allow anyone to stomp on my heart again, the way Greg had all those years ago. I had put all those feelings to sleep long ago, seven years ago to be exact, and I didn't want anyone trying to revive them. No heroics for this old heart. Just leave it alone and let it die of natural causes. At least it didn't hurt anymore. Cardiac euthanasia, I supposed.

Every time I start a new job, I force myself to get off the floor and have my dinner at a table like a civilized human being, instead of taking hurried gulps of food between watching cardiac monitors, signing off charts, and paging doctors. My resolve never lasts longer than the first week, but I always start out with good intentions.

It was only my third day back, so I was still intent on actually taking my allotted thirty-minute dinner "hour." I rounded a corner and entered the hospital cafeteria, which was now called the dining room in a pathetic administrative attempt to compete with other hospitals for patients, or "clients," as they were now called. The sign over the door and the furniture may have been new, but the entrée was still the same old unidentifiable chicken dish they'd served seven years ago. It might even have been the very same chicken, for all I knew. I watched passively as a morbidly obese, pimply-faced, young man wearing a chef's hat plopped the bland looking hodgepodge onto my plate. I paid for my poison and took it to a window seat in the far corner of the room, secretly glad that the six o'clock rush was long over and that I wouldn't have to be sociable with anyone. I just wasn't in the mood.

I was either temporarily spaced-out or having some kind of petit mal seizure as I stared blankly out the badly smudged cafeteria window. It wasn't until I felt a rather large hand trespassing on my shoulder, accompanied by a familiar male voice, that I was able to break my thousand-yard stare out into the sultry June night.

"Christine," an awestruck voice uttered softly.

Greg Anderson. I recognized his baritone even before turning around. It was a voice that, seven years ago, had sung me love songs, whispered X-rated sentiments into my eager ear . . . and dropped a hand grenade into my heart.

I knew I'd have to run into him sooner or later, I had just hoped it would be *later*. I hadn't prepared a speech yet, though I'd rehearsed at least a few dozen different versions during the endless ride through Texas on Interstate 10. None of them said exactly what I wanted so much to communicate, namely that no man had ever wounded me the way he had and that I hadn't been able to love anyone else since the day he pulled the plug on our relationship. I had watched from my window that day as he drove away, and I'd had to bite the drapes to keep from begging him to come back. I wanted him to feel very guilty now for his lack of commitment to me, but not guilty enough to rule out seeing me again.

"Greg." I smiled, doing my best impression of someone who has moved beyond the pain and on with her own life. I hooked my foot around the chair next to me and shoved it away from the table. "Sit down. Please." I beckoned with what I hoped was a new and alluring maturity.

He seemed relieved to encounter graciousness as he lowered his gangly six foot frame into the chair beside me. I suppose he expected the verbal daggers I used to hurl at him in the old days, but seven years is a long time, and I wanted to prove to him how far I'd come in all those years. Besides, I didn't want him to know how much it still hurt to look into those warm hazel eyes of his or that he could still hypnotize me with just a glance.

He was wearing the uniform of a trauma surgeon; green OR scrubs, blue, paper shoe-covers, and a matching blue surgical hat that did nothing to hide the unfamiliar gray hairs at his temples. Good. I was glad he had some gray hairs now. I hoped maybe he was balding too. Of course, I would have liked it better if he'd had an expanding waistline to go along with the gray hair, but his waist looked just as trim as ever, maybe better.

"You look great, Christine."

He was lying. I must have gained at least ten pounds since he'd last seen me, and the years hadn't been nearly as kind to me as they had to him. Surely he had to notice the little fine lines around my eyes that no amount of moisturizer could erase.

"So do you," I lied. Well, okay, maybe it wasn't a lie. He actually looked better than he ever had, but he still had some serious explaining to do if he had any thoughts of rekindling our relationship. I had no doubt it was safe to assume that passion like ours didn't just evaporate into space. In fact, I felt little stirrings for him already, and I was certain he must be feeling them too.

He began making superficial conversation, but I might as well have been in a soundproof booth offstage. I didn't hear a word of it. I was too busy flashing back to the days when Greg had loved me, or so I had thought. It was during his internship and I had been an experienced trauma nurse who taught him everything he knew. It was always like that with interns. They came on board so humble, so willing to learn, so respectful of nurses and grateful for the things we could teach them. By July 1 of the following year, however, when they magically turned into residents, they usually forgot our names and from then on, treated us like the brain-dead patients we cared for.

But not Greg. Our relationship had been very different right from the start. We had worked side by side every day in life-and-death situations, and panic had become a way of life for us.

It is common knowledge among nurses and doctors that there is something electrical, almost sexual, about working in emergency situations. The adrenaline starts gushing, body temperatures rise, and pulses pound. Add a little testosterone to the mix and you have a recipe for romance.

Something about those chronic adrenaline rushes and daily exposure to so much human suffering makes you face your own mortality, and it's not a pretty sight. You want to deny death and to confirm that *you*, at least, are still alive. You slowly notice that you are starting to lose the ability to feel emotions, and you desperately look for ways to prove that it's not so.

Greg and I reaffirmed one another's feelings and "aliveness" many times over the three years we worked together. We fell in love over an intubation tray one night when our forty-seven-year-old patient with an aortic aneurysm bottomed out on us. It was the first time Greg had ever had to intubate a patient without the reassuring presence of his senior resident. I tore open the tray for him and though we both knew I was far more experienced at this sort of thing, I stood back and talked him through the finer points of the procedure. Even then Greg had the "good hands" that would someday make him a successful trauma surgeon and he got the tube positioned properly, as efficiently and effortlessly as any senior resident. The only hint of his inexperience was the triumphant smile that glowed on his face as he reached for the Ambu bag and began bagging the patient as if he'd done this at least 100 times before.

After the patient was stabilized and we had time to catch our breath, we exchanged satisfied smiles and we both knew that some kind of meaningful bond had just been formed. He invited me to the little hole-in-the-wall pub across the street to celebrate when I got off duty at eleven thirty, and that's how the whole thing got started.

All of our senses seemed heightened by the

urgency of our work. Our admiration and love for one another quickly took root in the fertile field of crash carts, central lines, and ambu bags. It was the beginning of a three-year love affair, and it was all so passionately perfect . . . until the day I brought up the subject of marriage. That's when all the courage he'd shown cracking chests, running codes, and talking to malpractice attorneys, completely deserted him. Greg Anderson was obviously capable of great things, but commitment wasn't one of them.

Why he had never mentioned this little matrimonial-phobia to me three years earlier, when there was still a chance for me to get out with my sanity intact, I will never know. I do, however, suspect it had something to do with the fact that he knew how stubborn I was and that I would have ended our relationship right then and there had I seen him for the commitment coward that he was.

Greg said I was "headstrong." I said that's one of the reasons he loved me. He agreed, but he said that's also one of the reasons he wouldn't marry me. Of course there were lots of fights and dramatic overtures, but in the end, I threw up the white flag of surrender and left Valley Community Hospital and Greg. I hoped they'd be miserable together.

I'd just heard about a new kind of nursing called Travel Nursing, where you work for an agency and take short-term contracts around the country. I decided it sounded like the perfect balm for a broken heart, and I set off to live the life of a tumbleweed, drifting from city to city. Of course I ended up putting down roots in the first place I was assigned. Los Angeles looked awfully good to me after a lifetime of East Coast winters and the laid-back California lifestyle wasn't exactly repulsive either. But I'm going off on a tangent here.

Now, here I was, staring into Greg's inviting hazel eyes again and trying to squelch the little seeds of hope that were sprouting in my heart. That's when I noticed the shiny gold band on his left hand, and needless to say, my heart-stopping realization wasn't lost on him. I could see he was uncomfortable and, for once, speechless. He just smiled sheepishly while I gawked.

"Who?" I asked, barely able to coax the word past the lump in my throat.

"I don't think you know her," he said, shifting uncomfortably in the metal cafeteria chair.

"Try me," I challenged. I had to know, even if it killed me. It almost did.

He couldn't even look me in the eye when he said the name. "Anna Ranucci," he mumbled with an insincere grin.

"What?!" I was horrified. Angry. Destroyed. I couldn't halt the words that began spilling from somewhere deep in my gut. "You mean you wouldn't marry *me*? *Me* who loved you? *Me* who was your very best friend in the entire world? You said it was because you were afraid of marriage, then you go and marry some . . . some . . ."

"Hold it, Christine," he said defensively. He raised those engulfing eyes to look at me and simultaneously softened his tone. God, he still knew how to play me. "Look, you have every right to be angry. I understand that . . ."

"You don't understand anything!" I interrupted angrily.

He cut me off. "Look, Anna's a good person. You might even like her if you got to know her . . ."

"Don't make me puke," I warned as my fury

took over. Anna Ranucci? Of course I knew Anna Ranucci and he *knew* I knew her. She had been the staffing coordinator all those years ago, and Greg had heard me complain about her many a night. She never liked me because I was always threatening to call *60 Minutes* and have them do an exposé on the horrendous staffing shortages of Valley Community Hospital. Anna Ranucci?! She wasn't even pretty. She wasn't even smart. She was just a typically frumpy, submissive secretary with a fancy title.

Oh, I guess maybe that explained it. Maybe Greg was threatened by strong, intelligent women. He certainly wouldn't be the first successful man to marry a wimpy, brainless, subservient woman. How come I never noticed that about him before? Maybe I would have toned down my attitude a bit, had I known. Nah. What was I thinking? Besides, Greg had always acted as if he admired my rebellious streak. Had he just been humoring me for three years?

"I guess old Anna must have some *other* kind of talent," I said cattily, "cause God knows, she doesn't have a brain."

Surprisingly, he took that comment without

batting an eye. Obviously, he had decided not to fight with me no matter how insulting I got.

"Look, Christine," he said in his softest voice ever. "I'm happy now. Can't you just be happy for me?"

"No, Greg, I can't!" I retorted, embarrassed by the tremor in my voice. "And you'll excuse me if I don't send a belated wedding gift." I always resort to sarcasm when I'm feeling vulnerable.

"You still switch to sarcasm when you're feeling vulnerable," he noted with an amused smile. I hated him at that moment. Then I hated him even more when he added, "Look, Christine, I have *you* to thank for it really." He noticed the shock that must have registered on my face and quickly added, "I mean, if you hadn't fought with me and made me see how childish I was being about marriage, I wouldn't have been ready for Anna when she came along."

I couldn't believe what I was hearing. "Now I'm definitely gonna puke," I said, wishing there were more people in the cafeteria to witness my rejection of him.

Greg's beeper picked that convenient moment to go off, signaling him back to the OR so he could make more money than he ever could spend, simply for doing the work he loved. Some kind of masochistic streak emerged in me, and I dug hungrily for the sordid and painful details of his life before I would let him leave.

I learned that his bride of three years was now pregnant with their third child. Somehow, I couldn't picture Anna Ranucci pregnant with anything but bureaucratic ignorance (I refused to call her Anna Anderson—that was just *too* painful).

I pictured them making love in the master bedroom of an oceanfront mansion. It was a far cry from the steamy, passionate nights I'd spent with Greg Anderson in his stuffy little on-call room, between stat pages to the trauma unit. I even remembered how that damned beeper would go off at all the wrong times and how we laughingly nicknamed it "CI," short for "coitus interruptus."

The feel of Greg's warm hand covering mine brought me back to my miserable present moment and the fact that we both had to get back to work. He leaned in to give me a perfunctory little kiss meant for my lips, but I turned my head just in the nick of time, forcing it to crash-land on my cheek. I could have sworn I heard him chuckle as he strode confidently out of the cafeteria, and I wondered when he had lost the frenetic dash of the intern.

I sat there for a moment, immobilized by the intensity of my emotions and overcome with pain at seeing him again. Worse than the pain, though, was the slow realization that one ten-minute conversation with Greg had just completely erased the therapeutic effect of seven years away from him. Had I learned nothing in these last seven years? Had I turned my life upside down and moved a continent away, only to find that my heart had stayed behind?

I allowed the futility and the hopelessness of the situation to wash over me. Apparently the damage inflicted on my heart all those years ago was irreversible. It was like being in a Code Blue when everyone is working feverishly to save the patient and all you hear is that flat, monotonous tone of the cardiac monitor signaling that there is no electrical activity in the heart. It's over. Thank you very much, everyone, but there's nothing more we can do.

Suddenly, I was filled with rage. I hated Greg Anderson at that moment and I hated my pathetic life.

I needed a drink.

2

THE END OF MY SHIFT COULDN'T come fast enough. When the clock struck eleven-thirty, you would have thought I was Cinderella at the stroke of midnight. I gave the night-shift nurses a brief and hurried report, then bolted for the front door, leaving the mechanical melody of respirators and heart monitors behind in the darkened doorways.

I didn't care anymore. In fact, I hadn't cared about anything in a very long time. It was sad to think there was a time when I was so naively compassionate, I felt every twinge of pain that my patients felt. No more though. What once had been a bottomless well of kindness and empathy was now a dried up, empty hole. There was nothing left for me to give or for anyone to take. Tonight, the only pain I could feel was my own. This was the *new* Christine Moore. I was going to work at becoming more selfish. I was going to bail out of this House of Wretchedness and save my own miserable life for once. Let everyone else fend for themselves.

I slid into my '91 Mazda Miata and realized that I had more affection for my car these days than I did for any human being, past or present. I drove to a local beachfront pub where I knew I could have a quiet drink by myself and not have to deal with a bunch of rowdy New Yorkers, or "Bennies," as we natives liked to call them. Don't ask me why we call them that, I have no idea. Someone started it and the name just stuck. Of course, New Yorkers can't take a joke and had to retaliate by calling us "Clamdiggers." So be it. Summer tourists were the last thing I cared about tonight as long as they just left me alone with my misery.

My plan was to become pleasantly buzzed and push all traces of tonight's pain to some far corner of my brain. Then and only then, I would begin to make a list of all the things I'd decided to hate, men of course, topping the list.

The first Absolut and soda went straight to my head, since I hadn't eaten much dinner after spotting Greg's shiny gold wedding band. I pictured a massive destruction of brain cells with each sip of my drink and realized that if I was still thinking like a nurse, I definitely needed a second one.

How could Greg have done that to me? I had loved him with my whole heart and soul, not to mention certain other body parts. I knew I had loved him in a way that Anna Ranucci never could. Why did men always turn out to be such shallow disappointments? And Greg hadn't been the only one. Not by a long shot. There had been a long procession of insincere, selfish types who had both preceded and succeeded him. It's just that seeing Greg tonight—seeing him so damn happy—was the straw that broke this camel's back.

The bartender placed a second Absolut and soda in front of me, and I didn't protest. I must have looked like I needed it, sitting there assessing my empty shell of a life. Here I was, thirty-seven-years old and stuck in a profession that I didn't care about anymore. God knows, I didn't want to be a nurse any longer, but I also didn't have any interest in going back to school for a new and unrelated career. The whole thing just seemed like too much effort for a person who was as tired as me. In a way, I had let the nursing profession do the same thing to me that men had done, use me, drain me of all emotion, and then throw me away like a disposable instrument tray.

I glanced into the mirror behind the bar, and all I saw staring back at me was the reflection of a very tired and very lonely human being. Everyone behind me seemed to be in couples or at least trying to be, but I was content to stay by myself. I knew from all my psych courses that this was destructive behavior, but I honestly didn't care. I had no "significant other," and I wasn't about to go looking for one. Besides, what a stupid term that was. Of course, it was better than calling them boyfriends. I'd stopped calling them that the day I turned thirty. "Boyfriend" is such a juvenile term, and besides, by the time you're thirty, you're supposed to have a husband, not a boyfriend. I was already seven years over the limit.

Then there was my nagging little weight problem. Not that I would be considered fat by anyone's standards but my own, but the fast food hamburgers and lack of any consistent form of exercise were beginning to show on my hips lately. That made me even more miserable than I already was, if that were at all possible.

I took another absentminded sip of my drink and summed up my thoughts. I was a fat, misguided, lonely nurse who couldn't even remember what it felt like to be happy. Worse yet, Greg Anderson was trim, rich, happy, and married. It seemed the only hope of changing my life, in any minute way, was to give up the last two things I really enjoyed: men and fast food. Well, I could probably give up the men easily enough. That would be a lot like giving up migraine headaches. It was giving up the comfort and convenience of fast food that left me feeling unbearably empty and deprived.

I took another swallow of my drink, determined to enjoy some final guilt-free moments before beginning yet another stringent diet.

That's when an odd thing happened. I *felt* someone staring at me from the doorway. I couldn't see him well enough to make out any distinguishing features because the bright light from the entrance silhouetted him and shaded his features from my gaze. So how did I know he was staring at *me?* I don't know, I just did. Somehow there was no doubt in my mind that he was studying me under some kind of intense and unforgiving microscope.

I dismissed the notion and chalked it up to the alcohol permeating my brain cells. What man in his right mind would be looking at *me?* I had definitely let myself go over the years, and clearly I was isolating myself, putting up some kind of invisible wall that would make any man with an ounce of sense (if there were any of them left) move on to greener pastures.

Yet, even though I couldn't get a good look at him, what I *could* see was very appealing. Oh, probably it was just wishful thinking on my part, because nothing else made sense.

I was unaware at the time that things don't always have to make sense.

I got a closer look at him as he strolled toward the bar just as the band was finishing their last song of the set. He wasn't particularly good-looking or striking in any of the usual ways, yet he immediately stood out from the nerds, the drunks, and the desperados. Everything about him said "Cool," from his short in the front, long in the back sable hair, to his faded T-shirt and black motorcycle jacket with the sleeves rolled up.

Much to my surprise, he sauntered up beside me, nodded to the bartender, and in a voice that was slightly raspy, yet vastly melodious, he ordered club soda with cranberry juice. This not only amused me, but piqued my curiosity. The man definitely had *presence*. Against my better instincts, my eyes fell to his graceful hand, noting the coarse black hairs and the prominent, pipeline veins (what can I say? I can't stop being a nurse, even after a few drinks on an empty stomach). I watched him plunk a ten-dollar bill down on the bar and the nakedness of his left fourth finger did not escape me.

When his virginal drink came, I could have sworn he winked at me before tilting the sweating glass to his curvy lips. He set the half-full glass down in front of him and strolled off toward the band, apparently unconcerned that he'd left $7.50 in bar change just sitting there. He seemed to know that no one would confiscate his claimed territory. No one would think of it. He had a fascinating aura about him.

I couldn't be certain, but he seemed to engage me in some kind of momentary eye-lock as he ambled past. I was in no mood for male egos or for meaningless flirtations, so I quickly looked the other way. I'd seen his type many times before, and I was not the least bit interested. Curious maybe, but certainly not interested. I could read him like a book, and this was one main character I could definitely do without, unflappable, self-possessed, and dispassionate. The kind I usually end up falling in love with.

I have learned that I am an emotional diabetic and that men like him are Milky Ways, sweet at first but detrimental in the end. No sirree, I hadn't had my heart put through the shredder without learning a thing or two. Still, I was intrigued as I watched him casually greet the band members, and I couldn't help but notice the spark of recognition and delight in their eyes when they spotted him. I supposed he, too, was a musician of some sort since most of those types seem to immediately recognize the scent of a fellow artist.

I deliberately tried not to notice him anymore after that and turned my attention instead to my drink, which, much to my surprise, was just about finished. I didn't remember drinking the whole thing, but I must have. Tempted as I was to have a third, I knew better. As with men, anything more than moderation would give me regrets in the morning. Clearly it was time to go. I gathered my purse, left a fairly generous tip on the bar, and headed for the door, content in the knowledge that I had just averted another broken heart.

Emerging from the cool, air-conditioned atmosphere of the pub into the muggy, sticky summer night was like walking into a steam room. The Bennies would consider it oppressive, but to a native Clamdigger like me, nights like this are what we dream of all winter long. The hazy, pregnant, summer moon lured me across the street to the beach. I have always loved to watch the lazy ocean waves ebb and flow and sift themselves through the sand. I thought about how the Bennies only flock to the beach in the daytime, complete with gold chains too numerous to count, sun block, makeup an inch thick, and blaring boom boxes. Only the Clamdiggers realize that the beach is at its loveliest at night when the moon lights up the rolling whitecaps and the tide whispers sweet nothings to anyone who'd like to listen.

The early summer heat wave had driven a surprising number of otherwise sedentary people to the boardwalk in hope of finding a cool ocean breeze to punctuate the unusually high temperature. They spoke in late-night, hushed tones as they strolled the weather-beaten boardwalk, lusting after even the hint of a cool ocean breeze. Their voices were soothing and lulled me into quiet thoughts of my own.

How had I become so unhappy with myself and the way my life had turned out? Why couldn't I find solutions to the problems that were holding me back from a joyous life? I know for a fact that I am at least a fairly intelligent person and I've even known stupid people who are a whole lot happier than me. Why couldn't I find a way to fill the emptiness in my life?

Completely self-absorbed and lost in my thoughts, I walked the boardwalk with absolutely no idea of the marvel and the mystery that awaited me. I was also unaware of the loose board that was sticking up just in front of my foot. I stumbled on it and sailed through the darkness, striking my head on the cool metal railing and landing on my knees at the top of the stairs that led down to the sand.

My eyes scanned the darkened beach in an attempt to reorient myself from the fall, and I thought I noticed an odd form in the middle of the beach. I must have hit my head harder than I thought, because I could have sworn I saw a man sitting on a motorcycle, though I knew that was pretty unlikely. No self-respecting biker would ever take the chance of getting sand in his bike, so now I was certain I must have had some kind of head trauma.

I squeezed my eyes closed, then looked again. Sure enough, there *was* a man sitting on a motorcycle in the soft sand just beyond the boardwalk. As my vision cleared, I realized that he was perched atop not just *any* motorcycle, but a Harley-Davidson. The clean, powerful lines of the bike seemed to blend into the clean, powerful lines of his form, as though they were one, and from what I know about men and their Harley's, they *were* one.

The man and his bike were silhouetted against the backdrop of that huge, hazy moon, the kind that happens only in summer. The moon did its best to illuminate him, yet it wasn't quite bright enough for me to make out any of the fine details, like the color of his eyes or the texture of his skin. All I could see was a rugged profile of the kind of man you would *expect* to be riding a Harley. Yet something else caught my eye. Perhaps it was the tilt of his chin that emanated gentleness, rather than arrogance, and the smooth curve of high cheekbones that made him almost pretty. Though at first glance, he cut a rather intimidating profile, the more I studied him, the less intimidating he became. There was a sense of peace about this man, and I was intrigued.

Then I remembered what I'd decided about men just a mere twenty minutes ago in that bar across the street, and I dutifully chided myself. Here I go again, I thought, too romantic for my own good. I'm always giving men too much credit before they do anything to deserve it. I don't suppose I'll ever learn.

"Yes, you will." The words floated on the muggy air from his direction, and the voice was soft and kind. Even though the voice was unexpected, it didn't startle me. But wait a minute, it *should* have startled me. I had only been *thinking* that stuff and I was certain I hadn't said it aloud. How could he have heard me and why did he answer? Perhaps he had just been thinking out loud himself and hadn't intended his words to be heard. Sure, that was it. Just some crazy kind of coincidence.

His soft voice floated on the warm night air again. "Did you know that there is no such thing as a coincidence?" he asked. "Everything that happens, no matter how seemingly insignificant, is a part of the universal flow."

This was too much. "Who are you?" I demanded as I caught a flash of beautiful white teeth when he smiled.

"Don't be afraid," he murmured ever so tenderly.

"I'm not afraid of you," I shot back, a little

too confidently, given that I was still on my knees from the spill I'd taken.

He said nothing. He didn't have to. He simply offered his right hand and waited patiently for me to descend the stairs and to take it.

Me? Was he nuts? Did I look that stupid? This guy obviously had a lot to learn about women.

"Please," he said, in just the right tone with just the right mixture of kindness and gentleness on his face.

I was putty in his hands.

HESITATED FOR ONLY A MO-
ment, knowing I should be leery, yet completely unafraid of him. Me, the biggest cynic I
knew, being drawn to a strange man by some
unspeakable, indefinable force. I timidly approached him, never taking my eyes from his
gentle face as I all but glided down the weather-
beaten steps. I removed my shoes at the bottom
of the stairs, and the cool sand soothed my
weary, overheated feet. I stepped into the pud-
dle of moonlight that surrounded him, and he
extended his right hand more purposefully

toward me, though his body remained relaxed and comfortable on his Harley.

I recognized him as the guy from the bar who had been staring at me, the guy with the musician's cool. I bashfully shook his outstretched hand, pulling away as quickly as good manners would allow (don't ask me why I was concerned with etiquette at this moment). I know he sensed my shyness and apprehension, but he made no mention of it.

"My friends call me Joe," he said with a gentle smile. It struck me as an odd way to introduce oneself. Why not just say, "My name is Joe"? But then, I could tell already that there was nothing common or usual about this man.

"I'm Christine," I conceded shyly.

"I know."

Now, normally, considering the predatory climate of this little summer resort town filled with all kinds of lonely hearts looking for one-night stands, I would have assumed he was a Benny with a good line, but something told me I would be wrong. He was far too serene to be a Benny and far too sophisticated to be a Clamdigger. Somehow I just knew he wasn't even capable of using good lines. He simply didn't need them. Everything he said oozed authenticity.

"So why would someone with an ounce of sense park a beautiful bike like this in the sand?" I asked, trying to take the focus off myself. I was trying to sound confident and unflappable, like him, but I wasn't quite pulling it off.

"I'm not sure you're ready to know that just yet," he said in a velvety tone, through that ever-present smile.

Okay, now I was annoyed, not to mention slightly intimidated. Of course, the annoyance is what I chose to display. "Look, 'Joe,' " I said in a very sarcastic tone, "I don't really *care* how you got here. I was just making pleasant conversation, that's all. I really don't need this 'Mr. Mystery' act you're giving me." I turned dramatically on my bare heel and stomped back through the sand toward the safety of the boardwalk.

His voice wafted through the sticky night air again, sweetly and ever so softly, and his words landed on my heart as much as on my ears.

"Still a frightened little girl who has to show the whole world how tough she is, aren't you,

Christine? Still afraid someone might see through to the little cream puff inside."

I wanted to think I heard sarcasm or hostility in those words, but there was nothing but truth in them, and that truth penetrated my heart and momentarily turned me into a quivering jellyfish. I stopped in my tracks but kept my back to him. Who *was* this guy?

"Come out of the shadows," he invited softly. "You've already spent far too much time hiding in shadows."

I had this overwhelming urge to cry. How could anyone else possibly know what I thought only *I* knew, that I'd spent my life living far below my potential, afraid of stepping into the spotlight, afraid of truly blossoming? How could this man know all of this and why did he care?

I quickly decided that no matter how much he might think he knew about me, he couldn't possibly have a good motive. What man did? I glanced back at him one more time with every intention of walking away from him. Every horror story I'd ever heard of women being attacked in the dark of night, flashed through my mind, and every ounce of good sense I had told me to run far and fast. Yet something in my heart was drawn to him, and my feet began walking toward him without permission from my brain.

"That's better," he said, grinning.

"I don't understand," I murmured through a tightened throat and eyes brimming with tears. "Who *are* you and how do you know so much about me?" I hated the pleading tone I heard in my voice.

"You'll understand everything eventually." He smiled. "I'll answer all of your questions, even the ones you don't know enough to ask right now. Don't be afraid. I'm only here to help you."

His voice had me mesmerized, but something within me hated that I believed him. I knew I still needed to put on a show of toughness. "What makes you think I *need* any help? How could you, or anyone else for that matter, possibly know what I need?" I didn't like his superior attitude.

"Sorry about the superior attitude," he said, smiling a bit sheepishly. "I didn't mean to come off that way. You see, the point is that nobody else could possibly give you the kind of help or teach you the kinds of lessons that I'm about to give to you. No one else would even guess how much you still have to learn. Your act is actually quite good."

That made me feel both a little better and a little worse. I was terribly confused but, surprisingly, not at all frightened. There was a gentleness and humility about this man that even a bitter and resentful cynic like me couldn't help but sense. He had an air about him that made me feel safe. Something very deep inside of me knew that this man was not here to hurt me, that he wasn't even remotely capable of it.

He continued in his low and soothing voice. "You need to trust me, Christine. I know trust isn't something that comes easily for you, and that's no surprise considering all the near-fatal wounds your heart has sustained over the years. But if you don't give me your trust, even a mustard seed's worth, there's not much I can do for you."

The biblical reference wasn't lost on me, and I wondered if this guy was some kind of religious fanatic who thought he was God or something.

He chuckled good-naturedly, almost as if I had said the words aloud, which I was certain I hadn't. And then he told me things about my childhood that no one could possibly have known. He described in vivid detail the fear I'd had of Sister Mary Michael, my second-grade teacher in parochial school. He knew how hard I had prayed one night after losing my homework assignment that she would have a heart attack and die by morning. He described in frightening detail all the traumas of my rocky road through adolescence. He knew about the two times I'd experimented with drugs, and he knew that I now liked to relax with a glass of Chardonnay before going to bed at night. He spoke of all my old neurotic and destructive relationships with men and of the bitterness they had left in my aching heart. He knew about my love affair with Greg Anderson and how my heart had exploded into tiny pieces earlier tonight when I'd spotted the shiny gold wedding band.

He knew every detail of my life, every character defect that I had, every prayer I'd ever uttered, and every one of my heart's desires. When it seemed that finally he was through telling my life story, with details that even I had forgotten, I felt hot tears erupting from my eyes. I didn't feel so tough anymore.

"Who *are* you?" I asked again, in a mystified whisper.

He said nothing at first as graceful hands emerged from his jeans pockets and wiped the tears ever so gently from my face. "I am the 'God' you've been running away from for all of these years." He used his thumb to catch an unusually large tear that tried to slip down my face. "Some people really get turned off by that 'God' thing," he said, smiling, "so they use words like 'Higher Power' or 'Universal Force.' You can take your pick of what you want to call me. You can even make up your own name if that's what you'd like. Whatever you're most comfortable with."

"I thought your name was Joe," I said through my tears.

"I did. It is. At least that's the name I've chosen for this trip to this place. I took it from the man most people think was my earthly father. You know, Joseph of Nazareth. I try to leave off the Nazareth part though. It tends to make people a bit suspicious."

"I'm terribly confused," I whimpered. After all, I am a card-carrying atheist and I'd had too many old hurts and wounds and tragedies in my life to believe that there is any such thing as "God," especially a kind and loving "God." I knew better.

"It's okay," Joe said soothingly as he placed his forefinger in the little hollow above my upper lip. "Your reaction is only natural, but you'll get used to all of this. After all, you've been running in the opposite direction for a lot of years."

"Why do you keep saying that?" I insisted. "If you really *are* some kind of Mystical Being or Universal Force, you'd know that I've been praying to you for a long time. And that you haven't been listening," I couldn't help but add.

"Then how did I know about everything I just described to you? Especially all the prayers I just told you about?"

I stared mutely into his peaceful and lovely face. "You've got a lot to answer for," I said.

He smiled patiently and nodded. "We all do. We're all always evolving, getting better and getting closer to the real truths. Even me," he admitted.

"Even you?" I didn't get it. How could this supposed "God" person, or Mystical Being, or whatever he was, still be seeking answers and higher truths?

"I know what you're thinking," he said, "but no one is perfect. Perfection is just an illusion, a way of making you aim higher."

"You can read my mind, can't you?" I said.

"I prefer to say I can hear what you are thinking."

"Well, now hear this," I began with a little of the old spark of defiance back in my voice. "I want to know why you let so many of my prayers go unanswered. I want to know why you made life so hard for so many people, you know, starvation and disease and things like that. And furthermore, why did you lay down a bunch of rules that no one could possibly follow one hundred per cent of the time and then sell us a load of guilt when we broke those rules?" I was on a roll. I couldn't stop.

"You're referring to the Ten Commandments, I assume," he said with a pained expression on his lovely face. I couldn't help but notice that this man had the kind of good looks that sneak up on you. I really hadn't noticed them at first, but the more he talked, the more handsome he became.

"You bet your ass I am!" I'd been wanting to use profanity in front of God for a long time now, and it was worth the wait. It was immensely satisfying. Encouraged by his lack of rebuttal, I went on. "Those commandments were pretty rigid, you know. You left no room for being human or for extenuating circumstances. You know, times when a person has to at least bend the rules."

That said, I felt much, much better, even if I wasn't going to get any answers. The questions had been burning inside of me for a long time, and just the opportunity to vent them was almost enough.

Joe stared out into the night sky, both hands jammed deep into the pockets of his jeans. "This is gonna be a little more involved than I thought," he said.

Neither of us spoke for a few moments. I was thinking about how he didn't seem to feel a need to answer any of my questions or to defend himself against the heartfelt accusations I'd hurled at him. Then a funny thing happened. The ocean waves stopped rolling up to the shore and the people on the boardwalk became silent and immobilized. Someone turned up the brightness knob on the moon, and Joe and I were bathed in a spotlight of moonglow.

For the first time during our encounter, I was truly frightened. "I don't understand what's happening," I said, leaning closer into Joe and his Harley.

"It's simple," he said. "I'm getting you ready to live. I mean *really* live. Meaningfully." He turned his architecturally perfect face to the moon and continued almost absently. "You're right about the Ten Commandments. I was still new at this Universal Force business when I came up with that idea. I didn't realize I was being a little inflexible. Honestly, I just didn't understand then that one set of commandments can't possibly serve as a guide to everyone. We're all at different levels of our own development and evolution. What works for one person, certainly doesn't have to work for everyone else. I didn't know that then."

He turned to face me and I noticed that his eyes had taken on the same dark, murky color as the moonlit ocean. If I had doubted him before, I knew for certain now that this man was undoubtedly connected with the universe.

"That's why I've come back," he continued. "I want to reach everyone again and give each person their own customized set of commandments. You know, guidelines that will work for the individual, not the masses."

He placed his graceful, slender hands on my shoulders and locked eyes with me. "Right now it's your turn, Christine. That's what I'm doing here. I'm sorry it took so long to get to you, but I'm sure you understand the volume of work involved."

I stood there mutely, unable to respond to what I was hearing. I even began to wonder if someone had slipped something into my drink earlier and perhaps all of this was a hallucination.

"It's time now for you, Christine, to start a new life. I am the 'God' you've so desperately been searching for. I am the 'God' you sometimes think doesn't exist. I am the 'God' you think judges and punishes you. But you don't know me . . . and that's mostly my fault. Perhaps I didn't always make my presence known, but you must believe, Christine, that I am the 'God' who watched you grow up and watched you become discouraged. I tried to help you many times, but instead of trusting me and accepting my help, you chose to become angry and defensive. I understand that, but I hope you understand that I never stopped loving you and I never deserted you."

The earth remained completely still and silent, as if waiting politely for my answer. But I wasn't quite through chastising him. Talk was cheap. "So why now? Why did you stay away all those times when I *really* needed you? Why show up now? Now when I don't care anymore. Now when I'm not in a crisis of any sort. Now when I've learned to live without you." Then a terrible thought struck me. "Am I gonna die or something?"

His face brightened with amusement when he answered me. "Hardly," he said, grinning. "You're finally going to live. I'm going to show you a peace you've never known before. A peace so beautiful and fulfilling, you'll probably forget all about what your life has been like up until now."

"Good luck," I said sarcastically. I noticed an almost imperceptible frown cross his expressive face, and I regretted the words immediately. In spite of my determination not to concern myself with men's feelings anymore, I couldn't bear to see him hurt. "Look, Joe," I started again, "religion doesn't work for me. I spent too much time in parochial school and in church to have any faith left."

He smiled patiently. "I know how you feel about religion, and I admit it's probably my fault. That's where I got a little off track all those years ago. But people messed it up too. They misinterpreted almost everything I said and then even waged wars over who was right. It all really got out of hand." He looked at me solemnly. "That's why I'm here. To try to straighten out the whole mess."

"That's a pretty big job," I said, noticing that the world continued to stand still and probably would remain so until he had finished what he had come here to say. It was really impressive, actually. There was nothing to distract me from our conversation. I didn't have any idea how he'd done it, but it certainly was an effective communication tool. "Just how do you plan to accomplish all this?" I asked, completely taken with him.

"On an individual level, of course," he answered without hesitation. "Take you, for instance. I'm going to give you your own set of commandments to live by. Commandments that will make sense to you and that will lead you to the greatest peace you'll ever know. I have a separate list for everyone. Some people need more and some need less. It all depends on how complicated they've made their lives."

I was glad to see the old enthusiasm back in his eyes. "How many do you have written up for me?" I wanted to know.

"Six," he answered, almost before I finished the question.

"I guess I'm not as multifaceted as I thought," I said, trying to make light of it all. "Don't tell me you have them carved on two stone tablets and that I'm gonna have to climb a mountain to get them."

He didn't get it. "Oh, no," he said quite seriously. "It will be much harder than climbing any mountain. You see, I'm going to stay with you for a while. You know, hang around in your life till I'm convinced that you understand them. I'll watch you practice them a few times, and then I'll be on my way to the next person. That's how it works."

His face was boyish and adorable, and I couldn't bear to disappoint him. I was no longer doubtful about who he was. In spite of all my skepticism, there was only one person I could think of who could stop the waves in the ocean, brighten the moon, and immobilize the people on the boardwalk, and it wasn't anyone from this planet. "So how long have you been at it so far?" I asked. "—giving people their own set of commandments, I mean."

"Apparently not long enough. The work has really piled up. But I'm always learning, always improving—trying to get more efficient at what I do."

"Are you efficient enough now that I don't have to worry about you ignoring me again?" I asked earnestly.

"Christine, I know it's hard for you to comprehend, but it was *you* who walked away from me." His face remained soft and kind, but his words were firm. "Suffice it to say that I *have* never and *will* never leave you, no matter what."

I tried to digest it all as I looked down at his motorcycle and at the worn white, high-top sneakers. "Why did you come to me on a Harley?" I had to know.

"I had to get your attention," he answered simply.

"Why the T-shirt, the leather jacket, and the great body?"

He smiled easily. "I needed a new image. People today don't relate to the sandals and long hair anymore. They haven't since the sixties."

"So, just to make sure I understand you correctly," I began, "what you're telling me is that you *are* God, right?"

He understood my wariness. Apparently he had seen it many times before. He spoke slowly, choosing his words carefully so that my suspicious mind and hardened heart could comprehend. "I'm all that is good and kind and strong in the universe. I am the energy that makes seeds turn into flowers and flowers turn their lovely faces to the sun. Though I may be quiet and subtle, my presence is not to be underestimated. I am you and you are me. If you want to call me 'God,' that's fine with me. If you're more comfortable with a different name, that's fine too."

"I'm definitely not comfortable with 'God,'" I answered quickly. "I've spent a lot of time being angry and resentful of him."

"I know."

"I need a new image of him. One that doesn't automatically get spelled with a capital letter."

"Here i am."

"How did you do that? Talk in small letters, I mean."

"Christine, your mind is capable of understanding so many wonderful things. Don't squander that capacity by concentrating on old resentments and negative thoughts. There is so much good out there for you to learn. Trust me. Believe in me. We have a lot of work to do, but it won't feel like work, I promise. It will feel quite wonderful."

I was still reticent. Though my brain was completely convinced, my heart wasn't so quick to believe anything anymore. It had been disappointed and fractured and stomped on too many times for me to just naively trust anyone. Even someone who claimed to be, and certainly seemed to be, a Mystical Being. I still couldn't say the word "God." Of all the men who had let me down in my life, God had been the biggest offender. The biggest disappointment. I had never once felt that he had ever been on my side. No, even if this guy were God, I was still annoyed with him. I still had to make dumb, defensive jokes just to give my heart time to catch up with my brain. "Well, I've known a lot of guys who *think* they're God, but you're the first one who has me almost convinced," I said, smirking, thirty-seven years of sarcasm dripping from my voice.

He was too wise and too sincere to laugh at something that wasn't funny. His eyes glowed a soft brown in the summer moonlight, and everything reflected in them was beautiful. "Try not to be so afraid, Christine. And try not to be so bitter. Trust yourself. Let go. There's a wonderful life out there just waiting for you to catch up with it. Let go of the anger and let me show you the way."

"How do I know I can trust you this time?" I asked in a timid voice.

He put a long graceful finger over my lips and said, "Shhhhh. Do you hear that?"

I heard nothing and said so.

"It's the sound of some walls coming down. Walls that you've built around your heart. Do you hear them now? You've begun to trust me a little and the walls are crumbling already."

"No, I don't hear anything," I said obstinately.

"No matter," he said casually. "As long as *I* know they're coming down, it doesn't matter whether or not you hear them just yet. By the way," he added, "this is the first of your personal commandments. 'Do not build walls, but learn to transcend them.'"

"I don't get it," I said. "How is *that* going to help get my life back on track?"

"You tell me." He smiled patiently.

Oh, God, now he was going to make me work. "Well, I guess maybe I've built up some pretty powerful walls over the years," I answered pensively. "You know, walls to keep you out. Walls to keep me from believing in you, even though you're standing right here in front of me. And I've also used those walls to keep a lot of other people out too."

Joe nodded in agreement, but said nothing. I supposed that meant he wanted me to say more.

"But I like my walls," I insisted. "They've protected me. They've kept a lot of the hurt locked out."

"And they've also kept a lot of the fear locked *in*," he added. "That's why walls are dangerous. They keep you from seeing what is real."

"Okay," I conceded, "but what about that part about transcending them? Are you saying that now I have to break down all those walls I spent so many years building to perfection?"

"No," he said. "That would be too much work. It's much easier to just rise above them. You know, function independently of them. Just ignore them. It's not as hard as you might think. The hard part is learning not to build any more of them. Just keep concentrating on going beyond them, no matter how frightening that may seem at times."

I was confused. I had no idea how to go about

doing that. My walls had served me well and maybe I didn't *want* to let go of them.

"I know it isn't easy," he whispered, "but it's the only chance you've got if you want meaning and purpose in your life."

I stood there mesmerized by this man who promised to show me the way to happiness. I wanted desperately to believe him, but I didn't want to be disappointed anymore.

"I won't disappoint you this time, Christine," he whispered. His words fell on my heart like warm water on a block of ice, sending little rivulets of hope that streamed through my eyes.

"Okay," I sniffled, "I surrender."

Joe's strong, gentle arms cradled me against his muscular chest, giving me an almost primitive feeling of being protected from the world. All I could hear was his slow and steady heartbeat as my ear rested close to his heart. At first my nurse's mind assessed it as a normal sinus rhythm, but the more I listened to it, the more it sounded like the waves rolling up on the shore again. Joe smiled down at me, and suddenly I didn't want any more answers even though I had a million more questions. A cloud of serenity and peace had settled over me, and I wanted nothing to disturb it.

"I've always been so terribly afraid you didn't exist," I tearfully admitted.

"That's because you feared me and it was just more comfortable not to believe."

"But hurtful things kept happening in my life, and I always felt deserted by you," I retorted. "It just seemed logical to blame you for everything that went wrong."

He stroked my hair and looked up at the night sky. "Try to understand that when you blame me for things, you are really blaming yourself. Remember, I am you and you are me. We are forever connected and I shall never let go of you, no matter how hard you try to banish me from your life."

He loosened his embrace and cupped my face in those graceful hands, forcing me to look into his bottomless brown eyes. I was amazed at what I saw there. It was my own reflection staring back at me, but I was beautiful in a way that no fashion magazine could ever hope to capture. My face had the same peaceful look that I had noticed on Joe earlier. The tiny lines from all the old hurts and disappointments had been erased, and something nameless and lovely emanated from my eyes. I was speechless, and he chuckled at my amazement.

"You'll get used to it." He smiled. "It's called peace." Then, abruptly changing the subject, he added, "There's just one more thing that I forgot to mention."

I waited, not knowing what to expect.

"You mustn't discuss this with anyone yet. That's really important."

"But I thought guys like you, I mean, well, if you really *are* God, I would think you would want me to spread the word, so to speak."

"Not anymore. That didn't work real well the last time. It's like that game you play where someone whispers a secret to the person next to them and by the time the message gets to the last person in the circle, it's completely distorted. Well, when you do that on a larger scale, chaos and sometimes even war breaks out."

"I never thought of that," I said as I heard the sound of footsteps resume on the boardwalk. The ocean waves were rolling in again, and everything seemed to be back to normal. I spotted a Beach Patrol scooter coming toward us, and I mentioned to Joe that he might want to get his motorcycle off the beach before he got a ticket. He just laughed, but I didn't understand why. Of course, there were a lot of things I didn't understand, but I had a feeling I was about to learn an awful lot.

"Will I see you again?" I asked, not the least bit bashful.

His face lit up with an easy smile. "You see? You just did it!"

"Did what?"

"Transcended your first wall, without even thinking about it. You asked if you'd see me again. I know you wouldn't ordinarily do that with a man, even if you were dying to know. And it's walls like that which have been slowly killing you."

He was right, of course, and I was pleased as punch at how easy it had been to transcend that first wall. I could do this, I was certain. "Then there's hope for me," I said only half jokingly.

"There always has been," he answered seriously.

"I'd better be going," I said. "It's getting late and I have a lot to think about."

"I'll call you," he said, as I turned toward the boardwalk and the approaching Beach Patrol officer. It wasn't until I was locked safely inside my car and driving toward home that I realized Joe hadn't asked for my phone number. But he'd said he'd call me and I needed to believe him.

"That's what they *all* say," a little voice inside my head muttered.

TWO WEEKS WENT BY WITHOUT a word from Joe. I found myself just hanging around waiting for the phone to ring, and it annoyed me that I had regressed to such adolescent behavior. I had been completely taken with him that night on the beach, and try as I might, I couldn't get him off my mind. I tried to convince myself that I was just in some domestic phase and that was why I was spending so much time in my apartment, cleaning and rearranging furniture. Of course, I knew the *real* reason I was hanging around so much,

I just didn't want to admit it. Even though I had a perfectly reliable answering machine, I wanted to be readily available to see Joe again, if he should happen to call.

The call never came, and serious doubts began creeping into my heart, spreading poisonous resentment where only days ago, little seedlings of hope had begun to spring up. Deep inside, I knew it was time to be realistic. How could I even think he would call if I hadn't given him my unlisted number? And why hadn't he asked for it? Besides, getting an unlisted number should be a piece of cake for a guy who could stop the ocean and immobilize humanity and brighten the moon.

I began to wonder if the whole thing had been a dream. Worse yet, maybe it was something similar to a medical condition called pseudocyesis, where a woman with an overpowering desire to have a child, actually develops all the symptoms of pregnancy, including the swollen and protruding abdomen. She actually goes into labor after all this and then delivers nothing. There is no baby; there never was. It is only the mind forcing its deepest wishes upon the body.

Maybe I had been experiencing a form of this phenomenon the night I met Joe. Maybe because I so desperately wanted a man in my life and also because I wanted to believe in a fair and loving God, my mind had simply created them both for me. It hadn't been any more real than a false pregnancy. It couldn't have been.

I looked down at the mute phone leering back at me from its stand and realized how tired I was of men who said they'd call, then never did. I put on my sneakers and decided to go for a run on the boardwalk. Vigorous exercise always helped me in moments like this. It would lift my spirits and help put things back in perspective, not to mention the calories it would burn off.

There were a handful of die-hard runners on the boardwalk in spite of the unbearable heat. They were the same ones I see in the winter, running along the beach in blizzards and sub-zero temperatures. Apparently that "runner's high" is worth any amount of agony that leads up to it. All I knew about it so far was the agony. I stretched for a few minutes, then started my jog, breaking a sweat even before the first mile. For some reason, I was really enjoying the physical hard work, the sweating and pushing myself to the limit. I concentrated on nothing but getting into that glorious rhythm of a good run and feeling healthy and exhilarated.

To my surprise, I ran past my usual three mile mark and wasn't even winded. I continued on as I listened to the pounding surf, and I nodded acknowledgment to the runners who came by in the opposite direction. I must have run close to six miles before stopping, and I felt wonderful as the endorphins released by the vigorous workout coursed through my system. I decided to try harder on a daily basis to increase my daily mileage.

The phone was ringing when I slid my key into the door. I grabbed a dishtowel on my way to answer it and wiped the sweat from my face.

"Hello?" I said, a little breathlessly.

"It's about time you stopped obsessing about me and thought about your own well-being for a while," a melodious, male voice said into my ear.

"Joe," I said, unable to hide the delight in my voice. "Where have you been?"

"You mean why haven't I called. Say what you mean, Christine." He said it wisely and gently, not chidingly.

"Okay, why haven't you called? I was beginning to give up on you."

"I know. That's why I called. You sure don't give up easily, do you?"

"Not when it involves something I really want." There was just a trace of hesitation in my heart now. "And I want to see you again, Joe. I want to talk to you some more."

"I know. We will. But first you have to get any romantic notions out of your head. That's why I haven't called. I can't teach you the things you need to learn if you're going to confuse them with romance."

"Of course. You're right," I conceded, embarrassed that I had not been able to hide the fact that I was smitten with him. "It's just that it's been so long since anyone has made sense to me, or intrigued me, or had something worthwhile to say. You fascinated me that night and quite naturally, I want more. Is that so terrible?"

"Yes," he said. "It's terrible for you. It hurts

you. It puts you at my mercy. It keeps you hanging around the telephone when you could be out enjoying all the glorious things I've put here for your enjoyment. Things like oceans, sunsets, flowers, warm summer breezes."

"But you've got to give me *some* credit, Joe," I insisted. "I did put you out of my mind tonight and went out for a run and enjoyed some of those very things you mentioned."

"That's why we're talking right now," he explained as though he were speaking to a young child. "I can't penetrate your mind when it's filled with yearnings and romantic ideas. These lessons or commandments, or whatever you want to call them, are really important for you to learn. You have to be a willing student, Christine. Your mind has to be completely open to them, or we're both just wasting our time. Do you understand that?"

"Yes," I said honestly, but with a heavy heart. He apparently heard the disillusionment in my voice.

"Christine," he said tenderly, "the romance and love and relationships are all on their way to you. But it won't be until later. And it won't be with me. It can't be. That's not my purpose for being here."

"I understand," I said, though I was still disappointed. "But if all those good things are on their way to me, let's get started. We just wasted two weeks."

Joe chuckled warmly. "There was no wasted time at all, Christine. It simply took you two weeks to learn your second commandment." Then, before I could ask, he suggested, "Why don't you try to put into words what you think your second commandment is."

I thought before I spoke this time. I knew it must have something to do with not obsessing about romance and getting on with my life no matter what. "Okay," I started, quite certain that I would be guessing correctly. "Thou shalt not hang around waiting for the phone to ring."

"Close," he said. "But that's just a small detail of the bigger concept. Try again."

I closed my eyes and squeezed my temples, but the second commandment eluded me. "I don't know. Something about obsessions maybe?"

"Pretty close," he conceded. "Listen carefully. This is an important one for you. You tend to break this one a lot. Ready?"

"Ready," I said, not understanding how I could break a commandment that I didn't even know about, but I figured that was a topic for another time and discussion.

His voice was deep and resonant as he recited Commandment Number Two. "Live in the moment. For each one is precious and not to be squandered."

I was silent for a moment. There was no doubt this was an appropriate commandment for me. I had just "squandered" many precious moments waiting for Joe to call. I didn't even want to think about how many times I'd done that over the years with countless other men. I had missed a lot of sunsets and summer breezes and had been distracted from a lot of beautiful things going on around me in the moment. If just these last two weeks were to be converted into moments, I'd probably committed a mortal sin.

"Try not to think in terms of sin," Joe said sweetly into my ear. "You're here to learn, not to dwell on or suffer for the past. Forget all that sin stuff. That was another exaggeration of what I was really trying to say all those years ago. Forget about all that and just live right now, this moment and try to love what you see."

We chatted a little longer and I promised Joe I wouldn't obsess about him anymore. I was beginning to understand what he was saying. It certainly made sense. But how to train myself to live in the moment was a very difficult task for someone like me who wants to know if she'll ever get married or have children or lose ten pounds or own a house or at least a condominium. I admit, I think about the future. I always thought that was the right way to live. It was my idea of being responsible. If I was going to start living in the moment, I had some seemingly insurmountable changes to make.

"You can do it," Joe's voice reassured me through the phone. "But you've got to start practicing right now. When we hang up the phone, I want you to make a list of things about the world you never notice. Not big things either. Keep it simple. You know, everyday things that you tend to take for granted and don't notice anymore. Then I want you to water your plants and think about the way they drink the water up and how the water keeps them green and supple. Try to notice several new things every day, write them down if you must, and I promise you will begin to see your life change. Subtly perhaps, but it will change."

My mind was already racing ahead. I wondered if I would only have phone contact with him from now on or if I would ever see him in person again.

"You're doing it again," he warned, "projecting into the future."

"Well, I'm pretty new at this," I said a little defensively, "and it's going to take a lot of practice for me to get used to this 'living in the moment' routine."

"Perhaps, but it is one of the greatest gifts you will ever give yourself."

"In that case," I said, "I better go. I've got a lot of work to do. Goodnight, Joe."

I could hear the smile in his voice as he said, "They are *all* good nights. You'll see."

I heard the click of the phone on his end hanging up, and I sat motionless for a moment with the phone still in my hand, unable to stop smiling. I placed the receiver back in its cradle and took out my watering bucket. I filled it to the brim and began watering my array of plants that sat on the floor by the sliding glass doors. I noticed that they actually looked greener and healthier already.

Somehow, I wasn't surprised.

WITHIN ONLY A FEW DAYS, MY plants began to delight me with sudden growth spurts. I marveled at their new, vibrant colors and at their new eagerness to grow. It was even becoming necessary to repot a few of them. In a flash of revelation, I realized that my plants were only mirroring me. For I, too, was becoming more colorful and eager to grow these days.

It was the beginning of my noticing several new things every day. At first, I had looked only for dramatic things like magical sunrises and sunsets. Then I noticed how much simpler it was to notice the smaller things, like the way the seagulls all stand on the beach in the evening, facing in the same direction against the wind, so as not to ruffle their feathers. For the first time since childhood, I took note of the rattling song of locusts in the stillness of the summer night. I wondered how they actually made that sound, and I became so intrigued that I went to the library to look it up.

I began to see a whole new world evolve before my very eyes. A robin's nest in the tree outside my apartment prompted me to buy a bird feeder and hang it from the roof of my balcony. I even began to cook once in a while instead of dashing out the door for a fast-food burger. I sometimes rose early enough to witness the sun send its first flame-colored tip above the ocean's edge, and, try as I might, I never did glimpse the green flash that is rumored to appear just seconds before sunrise. It seemed that all of my senses were becoming more acute, and though I lived in a large apartment complex with modern-day conveniences including tennis courts, a dry cleaner, and a chlorinated swimming pool, it was the scent of lilacs growing within this cement jungle that I noticed most.

I studied simple things like my fingers and toes and marveled at their dexterity and the functions they served. I became very observant of all my bodily systems, respiratory, circulatory, cardiac, digestive, and I was awestruck at the efficiency of our human organs. How could I ever have taken them so for granted? How could anyone? It was like being a multi-millionaire and not realizing that you were rich. I thought about less tangible things like sleep cycles, dreams, and animal hibernation and was filled with a newfound reverence for all living things.

I took time at work to notice and appreciate the healing powers of my patients and I was humbled by it. Dressing changes on my postoperative patients were no longer routine or boring. It filled me with a sense of awe that an abdomen could be sliced open with a scalpel one day and, by the next, the skin would have already closed over the wound. I began to see these recoveries as small miracles instead of as a dull grind for me, and I felt privileged to be a part of it. Above all, I began to marvel at and appreciate my own good health and well-being.

My priorities were changing at an alarming rate. It was hard to believe that until this new enlightenment had struck, I had spent most of my free time browsing through shopping malls and fantasizing about all the lovely material things that I wanted. Now it was becoming unfathomable to me that I had overlooked all the "free" miracles and beauty that surrounded my everyday life.

Occasionally, I caught myself wishing Joe would call so that I could share my discoveries with him, but I quickly reminded myself of my second commandment and began living in the moment again, making it as lovely a moment as possible. Sometimes that meant smelling the fresh flowers that had now become a permanent fixture both on my grocery list and on the kitchen table. Sometimes it meant putting my feet up and reading a magazine or taking a shower with scented soap or writing poetry. Not that my life was perfect by any stretch of the imagination. I was still less than thrilled with my job, my nonexistent love life, and my weight, but my potential for happiness grew and developed every day and so did the pleasure-seeking mechanisms in my brain. I became more and more creative and found that it was entirely possible to routinely have a glorious day. If I ran out of ideas, I simply sat still for a moment (a miracle in itself), closed my eyes, and asked myself what it was I *really* would like to do right now.

Come to think of it, what I *really* wanted right now was a chocolate ice cream cone . . . dipped in that warm chocolate that hardens on the ice cream. Oh, yes, that was it. I slipped my feet into well worn flip-flops and stuffed two dollars into the pocket of my favorite white summer shorts. Normally, I would have had chocolate ice cream in the freezer, but not anymore. Normally, I would have driven six blocks to the nearest Dairy Queen, but not anymore. Now I realized what a lonely and compulsive thing it would be to sit in my apartment gobbling down what would inevitably turn out to be a quart of ice cream, not even tasting it, just trying to fill the emptiness in my life. I'm not sure why, but I wasn't feeling empty, just hungry for chocolate ice cream.

Now I would enjoy the walk as much as I would enjoy the ice cream cone.

A blast of cool air swirled around me as I opened the door to enter the Dairy Queen. I mentally added to my list how good that first blast of air-conditioning feels on a sultry, summer night. I bought my cone and licked the milky drippings as I scouted out a seat for myself.

That's when I spotted him.

Joe was sitting in the far corner, an untouched banana split before him, grinning at me as if he'd been politely waiting for me to join him.

"You're getting pretty good at this," he remarked as I slid into the cold metal chair across from him. I smiled. He continued. "So far you're an excellent student, Christine."

"Thanks," I murmured, truly more interested in chocolate ice cream than I was in compliments.

Without skipping a beat, Joe continued. "You know those plants in your apartment that you had to repot?"

I nodded, still licking the escaping drops of ice cream that tried to slide down the side of my cone. It didn't occur to me to ask how he knew I'd just repotted several of my rapidly growing plants. I guess I was beginning to take his miracles for granted.

"Well, you're a lot like them," he went on. "Pretty soon we're going to have to repot you. You're really growing at a much faster rate than I expected."

"Repot me?" I managed to ask. "What do you mean? Make me move to a bigger city? Really, Joe, I'm not ready for that. I'm really quite happy here and . . ."

"I would never *make* you do anything," he interrupted, "but don't kid yourself. You're not all that happy where you are."

"What are you saying then? That I should move or 'repot' myself somewhere else, right?"

"Relax." He laughed as he covered my unoccupied hand with his large, warm one. "You never have to do anything you really don't want to do." He scooped some whipped cream into his mouth and added, "Besides, that's not what I meant."

"Well what *did* you mean, Joe? Honestly, sometimes I have a hard time following you."

He rolled a piece of ice-cream-drenched banana around in his mouth, savoring the flavor and the tongue-numbing cold before letting it slide down his throat. I couldn't help but think that he was practicing the second commandment he had given me, the one about living in the moment and enjoying everything. Little did he know I had just about mastered that one.

He smiled a closed-mouth smile, and I knew he was reading my thoughts again. I knew better than to interrupt the moment and I waited.

"You've been doing your homework," he finally noted.

"Yes, but what's this stuff about 'repotting' me? You're making me nervous." I was being impatient and I knew it, but the thought of uprooting myself was very threatening to me. I had a feeling he was deliberately prolonging his answer in order to teach me patience, so I waited.

"You need to learn some patience," he said kindly, with no trace of chastisement. "But maybe it is time for your third commandment, even though you're a little bit ahead of schedule."

I said nothing and concentrated instead on

pushing the last of my ice cream down into the cone with my tongue, so I could bite the bottom and suck it out, all cold and soft, the way I remembered doing as a child. I knew Joe would teach me my next lesson in his own good time. There was no need to prod him.

I was just finishing the last of my gooey mess when Joe's voice seemed to fill the room in an almost mystical way. "Take care of yourself first and foremost. For you are me and I am you, and when you take care of yourself, you take care of me. Together, we take care of one another."

I was a little embarrassed as I noticed the man at the next table cast a strange look in our direction. Joe's voice could be soft as the rustle of a summer breeze or sonorous as the takeoff of the Concorde, and every range in between. It was apparent that the man at the next table had heard our conversation, but Joe paid him no mind. "Don't worry about him." He smiled. "He's one of the ones I haven't reached yet. I don't have him scheduled until five years from now."

"Okay, so I'm supposed to take good care of myself," I recapped, knowing that I would be quizzed on what he had just said.

"First and foremost," Joe added.

"Well, don't you think I do that? I mean I jog and I try to eat right and I don't smoke and . . ."

"And you spend forty hours a week at a job you think you hate, and you spend the remainder of your waking hours lamenting over how imperfect you think your body is and how lonely you are without a man in your life."

"Oh." I had no rebuttal. He was absolutely right. "Well, how do I fix any of that?" I asked a little self-righteously. "Besides, I don't *think* I hate my job, I *do* hate my job. *You* try working night shifts and weekends and putting up with doctors' egos and let me know how *you* like it!"

His smile was kind and knowing and ever-patient . . . and it really ticked me off. "You love your job," he said in his rustling, summer breeze of a voice.

"I *hate* it!" I retorted.

"It is part of your ultimate purpose here on earth. That's not to say it doesn't get tiresome or frustrating, but essentially, you *love* it."

"I hate it."

"You love it. But you do it in excess. You need to cut back a little."

"Cut back my hours, you mean?" I was incredulous that anyone would suggest such a thing, though I don't know why it seemed such a foreign idea.

"Precisely."

"How do you propose I pay the bills then? Unless, of course, you've come up with a way to survive that doesn't include food or shelter."

"Think about what you just said."

"About surviving?"

"No. About paying bills. What kinds of bills? Think about where most of your money is really spent."

I was getting irritated and it showed. "Well, there's the frivolous matter of paying the rent each month." My tone was sarcastic and I intended it to be.

"And is it really necessary for you to live in that giant cement jungle of an apartment complex?" he countered.

"It offers a lot," I answered a bit defensively. "It has a pool and tennis courts and a dry cleaning service."

"Try to be really honest, Christine." His velvety brown eyes held my complete attention, and if I'd still been holding an ice cream cone, surely it would have melted in my hand from the warmth that emanated from him. "What is the *real* reason you live there? What was the first thing that really attracted you to that complex?"

I had to think. What was he getting at? What was so terrible about living in a nice apartment complex? Didn't I deserve at least that much in life? Was Joe going to tell me that I didn't deserve to come home to a comfortable and convenient apartment after a hard day at work? Well, if he was, I was ready to part company with him right here and now.

"Your mind is wandering, Christine. Try to remember the reason you chose that complex in the first place."

"To meet single guys," I admitted.

"Why?"

"So I can fall in love and marry one, if you must know."

"What else?" he asked, ignoring my growing irritability.

"And maybe have an easier life, you know, not have to pay so many bills by myself." That answer surprised me more than it surprised him.

"Honesty at last," Joe said with a look of relief. "Don't you see, Christine, that you're not taking care of yourself by doing that? Your life would be far more fulfilling if you would eliminate your obligation to things that don't serve you."

"Well, I happen to think that having a roof over my head, serves me *quite* well."

"When's the last time you used the tennis court?" he asked evenly.

I was afraid he'd ask that. "Never played," I muttered.

"When's the last time you swam in the pool?" He was merciless.

"Well, ummm . . . I like to swim but . . ."

"But you don't like to get your hair wet," he finished for me. "Especially with the chlorine and all. It might make those fifty-two dollar blond highlights turn orange, right? And then there's the matter of being seen without makeup."

"Well, what do you expect? There are *guys* around," I answered weakly.

"So?"

"So I don't want them to see me like that."

"Why not?"

I hesitated. This was not only embarrassing, but painful. Joe studied me with encouraging eyes and I finally found the courage to answer honestly. "Because they might not think I'm pretty . . . and then they won't ask me out . . . and I'll just be a lonely old lady."

He waited a moment and then added, ". . . who never goes swimming or does any of the things *she* wants to do, because men might not approve of the way she looks while doing them."

I couldn't have said it better myself. I lowered my eyes and nodded my head in agreement. Joe reached over and gently lifted my chin with two long fingers, forcing me to look into that magnificent face as he added the bombshell. "And then you'll go around blaming men for your unhappiness because they are so shallow."

I knew he was right, but I still had some thirty-odd years of conditioning on my side and I wouldn't go down without a fight. "Wait a minute," I shot back. "Okay, so I pay fifty-two dollars every now and then to put blond highlights in my hair, but I do it because *I* like it.

And if men happen to like it too, that's fine. But I do it because it makes me feel pretty and *I* like that."

"Do you like sitting around the pool sweating? Trying to get the perfect tan so you can attract a man?" He was playing hardball now.

"I don't mind," I said, not too convincingly. "Yeah. Maybe I even *like* it," I added for emphasis. It was no use. We both knew I was rationalizing.

"Yeah, maybe," he answered noncommittally. "Then again, maybe you'd like walking along the beach with the sun warming your bare shoulders. And maybe the salty surf swirling around your ankles might feel just a little bit better than the chlorinated, chemically treated, pool water that you never go in. Maybe you'd even enjoy diving through a wave and bodysurfing to shore in the white, salty foam and breathing in the clean ocean air that only the seagulls seem to appreciate anymore. Maybe, just maybe, you'd like that."

Joe shook his head in a gesture of defeat, and suddenly I couldn't bear to see him without his annoyingly optimistic outlook. He looked like a little boy who had bought somebody a wonderful birthday present and then found out they didn't appreciate it. The world had been rejecting his gifts, gifts that he thought were precious. I knew I had wounded him by choosing artificial, man-made pleasures over the wonderful smorgasbord of delights he had laid at my feet. How could I have been so insensitive?

"Joe, it's not that I wouldn't *like* to live on the beach," I tried to explain. "I simply can't afford it."

"Not in the style you're accustomed to, maybe."

"What are you getting at?"

"That's for you to figure out." I must have looked confused because he added, "But I'll give you a hint. Ready?"

I was glad to see the return of his old sparkle. Torturing me with riddles seemed to do wonders for his sagging spirit. "A hint?" I said. "A hint about what? Repotting me, I assume?"

"B-11," he said, as though this would make some kind of sense to me.

"B-11? What kind of hint is that? B-11? What is it, some kind of airplane? Or machine gun or something? What?"

He just laughed and finished up the last of

his banana split. He gestured to his Harley parked outside the window next to our table and said he'd offer me a ride home on it, but it was probably better for me to walk so I could think about all we'd just discussed.

All the way home, I could think of nothing else. Maybe I really could cut back on my hours at work. Who came up with the idea of a forty-hour work week in the first place? Where was it written in stone? Just because forty hours is the standard, that didn't mean I had to abide by it. I thought about all of the things in my life that I had always believed were necessities, like blond highlights in my hair, and I decided it might cost a whole lot less to live with my honest self. Yeah, I was going to cut back all right. I supposed it could be done easily enough, yet I couldn't help but notice the guilt I felt at the thought of not working "full-time." Maybe Joe was right. He usually was. Maybe I could learn to enjoy my job if I didn't let it take over my entire life. The time had come to start taking really good care of myself.

By the time I reached the "cement jungle," I'd decided I didn't really need blond highlights or tennis courts or swimming pools. What I needed was *me,* the *real* me.

The evening newspaper was sitting on my doorstep as I approached my apartment. I tossed it onto the sofa as I headed for the bathroom. When I came back, it had fallen onto the floor but the classified section had remained on the sofa. I thumbed through it and an ad in the rental section caught my eye.

1 bdrm, 1 bath, beachfront cottage.
Vry affordable.
Must rent immediately. Call 555–7987

I looked at the page number and gasped. B-11.

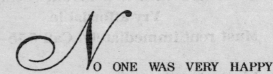

NO ONE WAS VERY HAPPY with me at work when I handed in my request to change my status to part-time. Everyone asked if I had started another job somewhere else or if I was going back to school. It seemed preposterous for someone to simply want more time to enjoy life. After all, they all still thought the only way to enjoy life was to make as much money as you possibly could and how could you do that working part-time? Joe certainly had his work cut out for him around here. They even tried to lay guilt trips on me, but I did my best not to let it bother me. I was bound and determined to take care of myself first and foremost.

The way I figured it, I could work two twelve-hour shifts and one eight-hour shift a week and still manage my bills—if I cut back on some of my expenses. I was more than willing to cut back a little if it meant more time to explore all the new aspects of my life.

For as long as I could remember, I defined myself by the work I do. Now when people asked, "What do you do?" I wanted to have a better answer than, "I'm a nurse." I'm *more* than a nurse, I must be. It was time to find out just what else I was. Joe had started me thinking differently, and I knew he was right. I wasn't happy and hadn't been in a long time, but I had been too busy to notice. The time had come to find out who I really was and what I really wanted.

Then there was the matter of the apartment. I couldn't believe I was giving up my little corner of the cement jungle and moving into an even smaller, less modern little cottage on the beach. But I was and nothing would stop me now. I was intrigued by the things Joe was teaching me about myself, and I had to admit that perhaps my style of living and my priorities had been a bit shallow. When you're as empty and unfulfilled as I was, it's easy to take risks. Nothing left to lose makes for bold moves.

I hadn't heard from Joe in almost two weeks again and I wondered if biweekly appearances were going to be his pattern. But then I knew someone like Joe would never be ruled by things like patterns. He was a free spirit and he seemed to bring out the free spirit in me, a free spirit I hadn't even known I possessed.

I was in the "beach house," as I liked to call it, on the first of the month, unpacking cartons. I couldn't imagine how I was going to fit all of my "stuff" into my new dwelling, since it had just barely fit into the old, more spacious apartment. Not that I owned all that much, but what I had apparently was more than the average beach bum had. And it seems beach bums don't need big closets. Where was I possibly going to put all of my clothing? I must have been out of my mind to think I could live here comfortably.

That's when a loving voice filled the room.

"Ego lies at the root of all your problems. Remove it and you make room only for happiness . . . and maybe even some of your clothes too," it added humorously.

I didn't have to turn around to know that Joe would be standing behind me, leaning against the open door and smiling that easy grin of his. It amazed me that he never startled me with his sudden appearances. Somehow it always felt perfectly natural for him to just materialize out of nowhere and spout something profound. I wondered how he did that.

"Your mind is wandering, Christine," he said, grinning as he stood silhouetted in the doorway.

"I know. It's just that you're always so full of surprises," I defended myself.

"You call this a surprise?" he teased. "You ain't seen nothin' yet."

"Well, do you have any magic that will make twenty square feet of clothing fit into ten square feet of closet space?"

I wasn't even mildly surprised when he said, "Sure."

He walked over to the bed, which was piled high with clothes, and began to sort through it.

Ordinarily, I would have been a little embarrassed, a little self-conscious, for any man to sort through my things like that, but Joe was no ordinary man. He held up a pair of my old jeans to me, the pair I'd bought two years ago when I'd gone on a crash diet and lost fifteen pounds. They had fit perfectly then—for about two weeks. I hadn't worn them since.

"You don't need these," he said gently as he dropped them onto the floor in what was to become the "get-rid-of" pile.

"Wait!" I demanded. "Those are great jeans! Okay, maybe they don't fit right now, but they will again someday."

"When?" There was no judgment in his tone, just sincerity.

"When I get back on my diet," I answered, perfectly logically.

"Diets don't work," he said. "Don't you know that by now?" Next he picked up the turquoise, strapless dress I'd worn to my cousin's wedding three years ago. Oh, what memories that dress held. I had met a friend of the groom that night and we really hit it off. We had drunk champagne and danced the night away. I'd had such fantasies of romance for us, and for a while

94

they came true until the night he gave me the same "I never want to get married" speech that countless other losers in my life had given me. At first I told myself he was only saying that because he just hadn't met the right person yet; he hadn't met *me*. It took two years of heartache before I finally realized he meant it.

"When's the last time you wore it?" Joe was asking.

"Three years ago," I muttered, as he held it precariously over the "get-rid-of" pile. "But it has such good *memories,*" I pleaded, as he let it drop on top of the size six jeans.

"Memories don't look good on you," he said, as his eyes crinkled in the corners and his lovely mouth sloped into a gentle, almost teasing smile.

The remainder of the morning was spent with me defending almost every garment before it ended up in the "get-rid-of" pile. Eventually, I had nothing left but my comfortable jeans, several T-shirts, a few pairs of shorts, and a couple of uniforms for work. Joe smiled proudly as he closed the closet door with room to spare while I looked forlornly at the pile of discarded clothes on the floor. Of course, what

Joe had saved was all I ever wore anyway, but somehow I felt deprived.

"Tell those clothes good-bye, Christine," Joe said with just a trace of a smile before picking them up in one armload and tossing them into a giant plastic trash bag.

"Good-bye," I said to the clothes that had been a part of my identity, my psyche. "What do we do now?" I asked, not really wanting to know the answer. "Give them to the Salvation Army?"

"If you like," Joe answered a bit distractedly. He was already looking through my box of tapes and CDs.

"If I like?" I repeated a little surprised. "I would have expected a different response from 'God,' or a Spiritual Being, or whatever you are. I thought you were supposed to encourage gifts of charity. You know, for the poor."

"You've already given a gift of charity—to yourself—by getting rid of part of the old you. You gave to the poor—the poor of spirit. Yourself. Anything you do with those clothes now is superfluous."

We went through my tapes and books and other belongings in the same fashion, discarding things I hadn't even looked at in years, but still had some crazy urge to hold on to. Joe pointed out to me that you could "outgrow" certain music and some books, and I had to admit he was right. Grudgingly.

Finally, everything was put away and the place looked neat and orderly. Actually, it was a little too neat and orderly for my taste. I felt a little depressed.

"Don't be sad, Christine," Joe said soothingly. "Now there's room for you to grow. Now there's room for the new Christine."

"I liked the old one."

"No you didn't. You've been empty and unhappy for a long time and you thought by filling up your time and your life with material things, you would find joy. But it didn't work, did it?"

"I guess not." There was no denying he had a point.

"This is all just an exercise in getting you ready to find out who you *really* are and what *really* makes you happy. You should be excited. You're about to finally start living."

I wasn't convinced. I still wanted to believe I'd fit into those size six jeans again and dance in a champagne haze in that strapless dress one

Joan Brady

more time. Most of all, I wanted to believe I'd
fall in love again, but the sound of Joe's laugh-
ter brought me back to the present moment.

"You're a tough nut to crack," he teased,
"but don't worry. I won't quit till I've convinced you there's a better way."

"I'm hungry," I said. "Let's go out for a bite
to eat." I thought how out of character it was for
me to suggest going out to eat to a man. Usually
I'd wait for them to suggest it so I wouldn't
sound too interested in their company. But Joe
was different. Besides, I was comfortable with
him, and there was certainly no need for pre-
tense with a man who could hear my thoughts
and who had just helped me organize my
underwear drawer.

"It's your soul that's hungry," he said, "not
your stomach. But let's go anyway. It'll do you
good to get outside."

As usual, he was right. My stomach wasn't
hungry, but my very being was yearning for
something that would probably not be found on
a menu. My soul, as he had said, appeared to be
malnourished.

I followed Joe out to his motorcycle, which
was parked in the alley between my beach

cottage and the one next door. The salty sea air invaded my nostrils, and I felt better already. Like a well-trained motorcycle mama, I waited for Joe to kick-start the Harley before climbing on behind him. I swung one leg over the smooth leather seat and rested my foot on the side pedal, careful to avoid the fiery heat of the exhaust pipe.

Joe looked back at me and smirked as he revved the engine. "I see you're no novice at this," he said with what sounded like admiration in his voice. "Maybe I won't have to teach you *everything* after all."

I smiled smugly and didn't say a word as I finished fastening the strap of the helmet he had handed me. I wrapped my arms around his trim waist and locked my hands across his flat belly as he popped the clutch, and we took off amidst flying gravel and the unmuffled sounds of a 1340cc engine.

As any experienced motorcycle rider knows, the passenger must have complete faith in the driver and the two bodies must ride as one. I'd had plenty of boyfriends who had criticized me for not being able to give them total control of the ride. They always said I resisted too much, that they could feel me pulling the opposite way in a struggle for balance, as we rounded corners and wound our way along curvy roads. Maybe they were right. I never was able to go with the flow and trust their ability. I remained hypervigilant no matter how many times they told me to relax.

Come to think of it, maybe I had done the same thing in my relationships with them. I was always afraid to give up control, even for a ten-minute motorcycle ride. But I was not going to make that mistake this time. This time was different. I really *did* trust Joe and I was going to prove it to him.

I closed my eyes and leaned into him, my face against the softness of his well-worn T-shirt. Riding with Joe was like dancing with a very good dance partner. The kind of partner who makes a novice look like an expert, merely by relaxing and following his lead. Joe was making me look like an expert "biker chick," and I stifled a giggle at the thought of it. If they could see me now.

Joe must have felt my suppressed giggle against his back, and he glanced over his shoulder at me and smiled. "I'm glad you're enjoying yourself," he called into the wind, and I felt the hard muscles of his stomach flex as he turned and spoke. I had no doubt that Joe was in complete control of the massive machine that carried us to our destination, and I had no desire to try to control things myself. I studied the shiny, straight black mane that fell from beneath his helmet and pressing my nose to it, lost myself in the fragrance of freshly shampooed hair. It was as though all of my senses had suddenly come out of hibernation. No detail, no matter how minute, escaped me. There was the sun glinting off his Ray Bans and the tiny lines that peeked out from the corners of his eyes as he squinted into the wind and sunlight. I studied the trace of black whiskers that were already growing, in spite of being freshly shaved this morning. I closed my eyes again and basked in the way the sun warmed us and the wind cooled us. It was a little slice of heaven, being with Joe this way.

I felt the bike take a sharp turn and slow to a halt. Apparently we were there, wherever "there" was. It could have been the Helmsley Palace for all I cared. I only knew I never wanted that ride to end, but Joe was revving the engine again in a signal that it was time for me to dismount. I watched him park and put the kickstand down as I removed my helmet and tried to fluff up my now matted hair. Joe laughed at my typically feminine primping and said, "Old habits die hard," as he hung both our helmets on the handlebar.

He sauntered toward me and casually slid a protective arm across my shoulders as we made our way up the front steps of The Surf Side Bar and Grill. "You're doing an excellent job of enjoying the present moment," he noted as he guided me through one door and then another to an outside patio. White wicker furniture was punctuated by oversized, brightly colored beach umbrellas, and we chose a table on the far end of the patio against the whitewashed railing. "Just don't hang on to those moments too long or you'll get stuck in them and miss the next one," he finished, as he pulled out a chair for me. Easy for him to say.

The patio overlooked a rolling stretch of beach complete with sand dunes and seagulls, and I wondered why I'd never seen this place before. Joe was right. Here was another very enjoyable moment, one that I would not have wanted to miss. Then from out of the blue, I remembered something he had said this morning as I was pondering my cramped closet dilemma. It was something about the ego being at the root of all my problems. I turned my glance from the serenity of the beach and fell into his waiting brown eyes. It was as though he had been expecting my question.

"What was that you said this morning when you first showed up at the beach house?" I asked. "Something about my ego," I added, straining to remember.

Joe smiled his easy grin and said, "I thought you'd never ask."

"Tell me, Joe," I pleaded. "I really want to learn this," I added a bit impatiently, though I really had no clue what this particular lesson was about.

"Okay," he agreed, "but please understand that your impatience is robbing you of the pleasure of living into the answer."

"What?"

"Never mind. Your mind still isn't disciplined enough to be receptive to that concept. It's better if we get down to the business at hand."

"What concept?" I wanted to know. I didn't

want to miss anything, but talking with Joe was sometimes a sensory overload.

"The one about living into the answers," he said, matter-of-factly. "But as I said, you're not ready for that yet. Let's talk about the ego thing first. Ego is at the very root of all your problems. Do you understand that?"

"Sort of," I said a little tentatively, too proud to let him know that I had no idea what he was talking about.

"Your ego is causing you problems right now," he said gently. "You won't even tell me that you don't understand what I'm talking about. Really, Christine, how can we possibly communicate if you're not going to be perfectly honest with me?"

"I think I'm being pretty honest," I said, pouting.

Joe wasn't fooled for a minute. "There's no such thing as being 'pretty' honest. Either you are or you aren't."

It was time to eat some humble pie. "Okay," I agreed. "I haven't a clue as to what you're talking about." And suddenly I understood perfectly. My ego had been getting in the way of progress without my even recognizing it.

Joe's face melted into a smile, and for the hundredth time I noticed how perfect his teeth were. "That's very good, Christine, now you're getting the hang of it. But don't be distracted by superficial things like your perception of perfect teeth. Keep your mind on the lesson at hand."

"Sorry," I said, no longer astounded or even mildly surprised at his ability to hear my thoughts. "It's just that I've always been a bit self-conscious about my own crooked teeth, so I fixate on people who have straight ones." I noticed the trace of a frown on Joe's face and decided to drop the extraneous topic of teeth. "Let me see," I said, on a more serious note. "If ego lies at the root of my problems . . . and I don't see myself as egotistical, then no wonder I haven't really resolved anything yet. But, Joe, tell me, how am I egotistical? I mean besides the fact that I didn't want you to think I was too dumb to understand what you were trying to teach me."

"There's an important lesson in that example," he warned. "Don't be too quick to discard it."

My next thought was interrupted by the

appearance of a very young and very leggy waitress. She wore white short shorts that did nothing to dull the tan on her magnificent legs and a yellow halter top that did nothing to hide what was beneath it. She smiled at Joe, and I tried to ignore the fact that even her teeth were perfect too. Without taking her eyes off Joe, she asked if he was ready to order. I didn't like the way he smiled at her and the way she maintained direct eye contact with him as I ordered my BLT on rye with just a smear of mayonnaise. She didn't ask what I wanted to drink, but she catered to Joe's every whim as he ordered a cheeseburger, fries, and coke. I didn't like it one bit.

Joe watched our willowy waitress sashay back to the kitchen with our orders. He finally turned back to me and nonchalantly asked, "So what do you think?"

"I think she's hot for you," I said. "And I think she should learn some manners," I added before I could stop myself.

"Not what do you think about *her*," he said, laughing. "What do you think about *you*?"

Then it hit me like a ton of bricks. Right in the ego. I was jealous! And my own self-absorption was to blame for this miserable feeling. "I guess I *am* egotistical," I said in quiet amazement, still uncomfortable with this unfamiliar image of myself.

"Don't worry," Joe said kindly, as he cupped my folded hands in both of his. "The hardest part is admitting to it. After that it gets easier." Then those brown velvet eyes of his took on a teasing glint as he added, "You *did* ask for another example."

I couldn't believe it. Joe had just conjured up the whole flirting waitress incident in order to provide me with another example of my unleashed vanity. Was there no limit to this man's power?

"So besides this whole ego thing," I said pensively, "the lesson here was that if I didn't want so much to be the apple of your eye, you wouldn't have the ability to hurt me, right?"

"Something like that," he said with a nod. "The main point is to live honestly with yourself, so that no one and nothing threatens you."

"That sounds like a pretty tall order to me," I returned, feeling a bit overwhelmed with all I had yet to learn.

He leaned forward and his eyes took on an

intensity I'd not seen before. "Christine, if you know exactly who and what you are, complete with shortcomings as well as talents, then you never have to waste your time or energy trying to be anything else." He paused long enough to be certain I was digesting what he said. "And the next step," he went on, "is to embrace your shortcomings and wallow in your talents and to love everything that is you." He was quiet again for a moment, before adding his conclusion. "The way *I* love you," he said, lips curved into a gentle smile and liquid eyes shining with sincerity.

I gulped, unable to make any other sound come out of my throat. Joe loved me? Was it possible? Of course it was. Joe wouldn't lie. He wouldn't waste his time or energy on lies, unlike most guys I knew.

What I couldn't understand was why Joe had said he loved me but had also told me earlier that romantic love would come later and that it wouldn't be with him. Well, maybe he had changed his mind. He'd changed his mind about a lot of other things, like his approach to the Ten Commandments, so why couldn't he change his mind about his relationship with me?

I studied the face of this man who said he loved me, looking for lies but hoping for truth. The sky had turned orange with the glow of approaching sunset, and it tinted Joe's bronzed face with a glow not unlike the special effects of a movie.

"This isn't a movie, Christine," he said, locking his eyes with mine. "You look just as lovely in this gentle light, as you think I do. Because you *are* me. And I, of course, am you."

"B-but, you said I shouldn't fall in love with you," I said hesitantly.

"That's right," he answered, shooting a poisoned arrow straight into my heart. "But that doesn't mean you shouldn't love me. In the purest, most unspoiled way," he added. "The way I love you."

The poison arrow was neutralized and fireworks were exploding again in my heart. Now I understood. This was *real* love, the kind I'd always been searching for. The kind that had been within me all along. Realizations began sweeping over me like a bolus of epinephrine shot through an intravenous line. All those heartaches! All that unrequited love in past relationships! It had all been so unnecessary, and now I saw it all so clearly. All I'd ever had to do was see myself for who I was, *love* myself for who I was, then simply share that love. Whether or not it was returned didn't matter. It was only important that I allow myself to *really* feel something, really love, with no need for anything in return. Why hadn't I seen this years ago? How much heartache I could have saved myself!

Joe tightened his grip around my hands and said, "You see, all along it was your ego that prevented you from really loving. You didn't want to give anything unless there was a guarantee that you'd get something back. You still didn't know that the real joy is in the giving."

"But what about people who take advantage of that?" I wanted to know. "People who are greedy and who take all you have to offer, but they never give anything in return?" I trusted Joe with my heart and soul, but as for the others of his gender, I still had serious reservations.

"They can't take advantage of something you

don't give them," he said. "Give them your love, but don't ever give them your very self. That only belongs to you."

Okay. That made sense. But I still wasn't satisfied. After all, wasn't that what marriage was all about? About giving yourself completely to someone? Was Joe saying that marriage didn't really work? The statistics certainly backed him up.

Naturally, he heard my thoughts. He let go of my hands, pushed himself back in his chair, and studied me from across the table, completely ignoring the cheeseburger the waitress had just put in front of him. "Marriage does work, Christine," he said earnestly. "You'll find that out soon enough. But it only works between two people who have slain their own dragons and who understand that real love is what grows in a heart that has been fertilized with the seeds of self-awareness and a heart that is strong enough to sustain that hard-earned sense of self."

It made perfect sense. No wonder relationships had never worked for me in the past. I had been using them as a quick fix; a Band-Aid solution for the hard work that I really needed to do. What I had really needed all these years was the courage to look at myself honestly. And of course, that would have required letting go of my ego.

Joe was staring at me when I finally snapped out of my daze. The orange glow of sunset had intensified, and now everything was enveloped in those soft and subtle flame-colored shades of evening. The sand, the sky, and even the ocean waves that lapped gently on the hard-packed sand of low tide were bathed in those muted colors of the dying sun. Joe watched the light show with pride and waited patiently for the question he knew was burning in my brain.

"Are there really men out there who understand the real meaning of love?" I asked, certain that there couldn't be. After all, I'd dated an awful lot of men and none of them had even hinted at this kind of discussion.

"Some," Joe conceded.

"Some? How many? Where can I find one?" Suddenly I was excited. I had to find one. Time was running out.

"Hold your horses," Joe said, chuckling. "I must admit that there are more women than men who understand the concept of true love.

Women are just more perceptive that way. But there are some men who understand it too."

"Where are they?" I asked enthusiastically.

Joe shook his head in amusement. He pulled his plate back in front of him and began to devour the now cold cheeseburger. Eating my cold BLT was the last thing on my mind, but I knew better than to hurry Joe when he was about to teach me something.

"They're everywhere," he finally answered.

"Be specific," I pleaded. "Is there one in this restaurant right now?" I wanted to know as I scanned the patrons from this mellow little beach community.

"Um hmmm," he answered without looking up from his burger.

"Well, which one is he? How do I approach him?" I was impatient to make up for lost time.

Joe patted delicately at the corners of his curvy mouth with the tip of his napkin with maddening slowness. "You don't approach *him,*" he finally answered. "It's more complicated than that."

"Well then, how do I meet him?"

"You *attract* him. It's much more effective than approaching him."

"But you made me get rid of all my really hot looking clothes," I whined. I hate it when I whine.

"Not *that* way." He smirked, continuing to eat that damned burger. "That's your ego getting in the way again."

Damn. He was right, as usual. Would I ever learn? "Well, if I can't appeal to his hormones, what *do* I use to appeal to him?" Just as I asked the question, I realized the answer, but Joe beat me to the punch.

"You use an honest heart," he said. "You simply be yourself. Your real self. You start doing the things you really enjoy, doing them every day, several times a day if you like. You wear the clothes that make you feel most comfortable and most like yourself. You listen to the kind of music that truly moves you. You trust your body to tell you what to eat instead of trying to adhere to some crazy diet. Eventually, an enlightened man will catch all the vibrations that emanate from your contented soul and BAM!—he somehow shows up on your doorstep. It's as easy as that."

"But how does he find me?" I couldn't afford to take any chances.

"That's for him to figure out. You don't need to spend your time learning what another species needs for survival. Just concentrate on your own survival and the rest will fall into place." He caught my doubtful look and added, "I *promise*."

By the time I crawled into bed that night, my head was spinning from all that Joe had taught me. I didn't want to forget even the slightest detail of the day's lesson and so I decided to write the essence of our conversation in my journal. I didn't want to trust my memory on something this important.

I jumped out of bed and sat at my desk, facing the waxing moon that lit up the tiny room. As the ocean hummed its soothing lullaby outside my window and the moon spilled its iridescent glow onto the paper, I wrote:

DROP THE EGO. BE REAL.

AND WATCH WHAT HAPPENS.

7

IN THE DAYS THAT FOLLOWED, A curious thing began to happen. I noticed that I actually seemed to enjoy my job. I even caught myself smiling from time to time, and no one was more baffled by that than me. I had been stimulated by my job at times and very challenged by it at others, but as far back as I could remember, I had never *enjoyed* it. I didn't think you were supposed to. Ever since cutting back on my hours (not to mention cutting back on my income), I was not as all-consumed by my job as I once had been. Work had become just another small part of my ever more interesting life. Or maybe *I* was becoming more interesting.

Learning to leave my ego out of my everyday life turned out to be the most important lesson I'd learned so far. Somehow I had taken the blinders off and the world around me became a fascinating place. I no longer saw my physical appearance or the image I projected as the center of the universe. Instead, I grew intrigued with more important questions, like what the people who scan the beach with metal detectors were finding. I checked out what the fishermen were catching, and I realized that seagulls open clams by dropping them on the rocks. Instead of reading women's magazines with the endless articles on how to be beautiful and sexy, I read newspapers and learned about world events. I already *knew* I was beautiful and sexy simply because I exist. Most surprising of all, I was able to pass a mirror without needing to reassure myself that I looked all right. I didn't need to criticize myself anymore. I was too busy finding ways to enjoy myself.

My favorite discovery of late was the saxophone music of a local musician named Jim

MaGuire. I happened to hear his latest and little-known CD while I was browsing through a beachfront music store during my now abundant free time. I had intended to buy some soft rock, something like Kenny Loggins or Carly Simon, but the haunting notes of that saxophone wafted through the store's speakers and hypnotized me. Something in the music touched me in my very soul and turned it liquid. It made me want to dance and flow like an undiscovered mountain stream.

I'm certain that the teenage clerk immediately classified me as an old fogey or a nerd when I asked him where I could find that particular CD. I didn't mind. Things like that didn't bother me since I had learned to leave my ego behind. I had no need to be considered "cool" by anyone, and it was a lovely feeling. I couldn't wait to get home so I could sway and dance to the music in private. I wouldn't even have cared if the one piece I'd heard in the music store was the only good one on the whole CD.

I stopped at the grocery store on the way home, since I knew the refrigerator was practically empty. It amused me to realize how unstructured I'd become lately. In the old days, before Joe breathed life into my life, I worked forty hours a week and had designated Monday as grocery night and Thursday as laundry night. I would never have allowed the refrigerator to get empty or the laundry to pile up, but things like that didn't seem so important anymore. These days I spent less time at work and doing chores and more time discovering the world around me. Sometimes I was astounded to find that I had *forgotten* to eat, which is something that I had never dreamed possible.

I kicked the door closed with my foot as I entered my little beach cottage with arms full of groceries. I unpacked Jim MaGuire's saxophone music first and popped it in the CD player, even before putting away the frozen yogurt. I certainly had my priorities straight. I rocked gently on my toes in time with the soothing strains of music as I whipped up a creative salad. Never in my life had I craved vegetables, but for some reason lately, all kinds of new appetites were springing up in my life. Usually I only made salads when I was punishing myself for being a few pounds over my idea of ideal weight, but now I really *wanted* a salad.

That had never happened before, and from the fit of my "racer red" running shorts, I'd apparently lost a few pounds lately without even noticing it. And *that* had certainly never happened before.

I lit the two vanilla candles I had bought at the grocery store and poured a glass of Chardonnay, which I never got around to drinking. I closed my eyes and wrapped both arms around myself and drank in the music of Jim MaGuire instead. I rocked gently at first, swaying and dancing to music that flowed like summer sunshine into the darkened caverns of my heart. I was completely engrossed in the loveliness of the moment, and when Jim MaGuire coaxed his horn to an almost impossibly high note, I swirled past the hide-a-bed sofa . . . and into a pair of tanned and muscular arms.

"Joe," I murmured, eyes still closed, not at all surprised to find him dancing in the living room with me. I didn't understand how I even knew it was him without opening my eyes, but I did know that none of that mattered right now.

He said nothing. He just drew me close to him in perfect rhythm to the music and placed his well-defined chin on the top of my head. My ear rested against his muscular chest, like the first time I'd met him, and once again, I heard the ocean waves instead of a heartbeat. I peeked at those rugged, masculine arms holding me and felt an overwhelming sense of well-being, as though I were protected from all possible harm.

He pulled me close until I was one with him. My feet were his feet and we drifted languorously and in perfect synchrony to the mellow and fading musical creation of Jim MaGuire. I don't know how I knew exactly which steps to take, but I knew better than to ask questions like that. When Joe was around, it seemed anything was possible.

"All things are possible all of the time," Joe murmured silkily into my ear. "And there is never a time when I am not with you. There are only times when you lose your awareness that I am with you."

There was no need for a reply on my part. There was no need for anything, in fact. I simply allowed myself to melt into him and to be one with this . . . this . . . Being. We flowed to the music, and when the final haunting notes of the saxophone hung in the air then floated off in the distance as the piece ended, my heart was overwhelmed with emotion. I knew it was against all the rules, but I was in love with this man. Hopelessly and helplessly in love with him.

Wordlessly, Joe guided me to the plush cushions of my cream-colored couch, and we sank into its accepting embrace, my head still against his strong and protective shoulder. Tears pushed their way to the forefront of my eyes, then overflowed down my face. They were tears of some unnamed feeling, not sad tears, but joyful ones. I quickly buried my face in his chest, embarrassed by my lack of restraint and ashamed of my runaway emotions. "I'm sorry" was all I could offer as an explanation for this childish outburst.

Graceful fingers stroked and explored my hair and a tender kiss was woven into my tresses. "Never apologize for being who you really are. For showing what you really feel," he said into my hair, his breath warm against my scalp.

Oh, God, how had this happened? How could I be falling in love with *God?* It must be against some kind of very basic rule. Leave it to me. I was probably looking at some serious time spent in hell for this one, yet somehow it didn't matter. How could this kind of love ever be wrong?

I pulled away and lifted my tear-streaked face to him. "I love you, Joe," I whispered. "And that's against all the rules we agreed upon," I painfully admitted.

Joe studied me silently for a long moment, and then those bottomless brown eyes took on an amused glint and he said in a perfect "Joisey" accent, "Yeah, so?"

I was dumbfounded. I had expected a lecture and what I got instead was a green light. I started to say something, but Joe quickly put his finger over that little hollow above my lip and quieted me.

"Christine," he said softly, eyes shining, "don't you see? It's perfectly all right for you to love me. It's your *interpretation* of what you're feeling that's a little off base. But the basic feeling is right on target."

I stared at him blankly. As usual, I hadn't a clue what this was all about. "I think maybe you need to put me in a remedial class," I said exasperated with my inability to understand the things that Joe tried so patiently to teach me.

Joe's laugh was as fluid as the saxophone music in the background. "You're being awfully hard on yourself, don't you think?"

"But I don't get it, Joe," I complained. "I thought we agreed that I wasn't supposed to have any romantic notions about you. And now I've gone and blown it all by letting myself fall madly in love with you."

He cupped my face in those large, graceful hands and held my gaze with his fathomless, mahogany eyes. I thought maybe for once, *I* was hearing *his* thoughts because I didn't see his lips move, but I heard his voice as clear as a seagull's song when the wind is blowing in just the right direction. "It's not that way at all, Christine," he was saying. "What you're feeling for me is real. Very real. But you're calling it by the wrong name."

"What am I calling it?"

"Romantic love."

"So what is it, really?"

"It's genuine love. Love in its purest form. The kind that just wants to be expressed. The kind that asks for nothing in return. The kind you've been searching for all of your life."

He was right, of course. Was this man *ever* wrong? This was exactly the kind of love he'd described to me the other day at lunch. Now he was providing me with an example. Clearly there was no crime in loving Joe this way. I wanted nothing from him but the opportunity to express the feelings that he dug down and pulled out of me. It was all right to love Joe this way. In fact, it was the most natural thing in the world when you really thought about it. After all, he was me and I was him. Our very souls were somehow intertwined and this kind of unselfish love was the very genuine result of that special connection between us.

For once in my life, I was experiencing the real thing. Incredibly, there was no pain. What a concept! Love, real love, doesn't hurt. Suddenly I was filled with an overwhelming sense of myself. Of magnanimous love for myself. It didn't matter how I looked or what I accomplished in this life, I LOVED MYSELF! For the first time. Finally.

I turned my gaze back to Joe to share this magnificent insight, but he wasn't there anymore. Disappeared into thin air, I supposed. I rose from the couch as though in a trance, and in a way, I suppose I was. I wasn't the least bit unsettled by Joe's mysterious comings and goings anymore. I walked over to the mirror on the wall and I saw Joe staring back at me. I laughed. He laughed.

"I finally love myself, Joe," I said, beaming.

"I know," he said, proud as a peacock.

8

IT WASN'T LONG AFTER THAT night that I saw an ad in the local newspaper advertising that Jim MaGuire was playing his seductive saxophone in one of the many infamous nightclubs that line the Jersey shore. New Jersey's reputation may take a powerful beating at times, but no one in their right mind would deny that our music scene is anything less than "happening." Of course, we have Bruce Springsteen to thank for that.

And if Springsteen was "The Boss," then Jim

MaGuire was "The Sauce." The icing on the cake. The Crème de la Crème.

I sneaked out of work early that night and paid a ten-dollar cover charge to see the man behind the saxophone who so intrigued me.

It felt like entering a cave at first. The room was dark and smoky and at least ten degrees cooler than the muggy summer night outside. The only illumination came from some red and blue neon Budweiser signs in the shape of a can of beer under a palm tree. There were three or four of them hanging on the far wall and they cast an eerie glow on the faces of the mellowed out crowd.

Arriving at midnight like this reminded me of younger years when it was considered "uncool" to be seen anywhere before the twelve o'clock hour. For some reason, I seemed to fit right in tonight. Before meeting Joe, I would probably have been overdressed on a night like this, but he had taught me well. By encouraging me to get rid of all my old "hot" outfits when I moved into my little beach house, I now had little choice as to what I would wear for any occasion.

Like most seasoned three-to-eleven nurses, I

had thrown some civvies into a knapsack and kept it in my locker at the hospital. I actually felt my whole mood shift gears when I stripped off my white uniform in our musty locker room and slid into my comfortable old jeans, white T-shirt, and white high-top sneakers. I had washed my face with cold water and applied some confiscated hospital lotion to my sun-kissed face. I didn't use much makeup these days, since my face had a warm glow from long morning walks on the beach and my eyes reflected a peaceful and contented soul. What would be the point in painting over that?

With my comfortable clothes and almost makeupless face, I looked and felt like someone who really belonged in this artsy, mellow, musical scene. The trick of fitting in, I had discovered, was in not trying to fit in. I proved my point by ordering a bottle of mineral water. I no longer had any need to alter my mental state with alcohol. Real life was infinitely more interesting and more exciting.

The cool water glided down my throat and sent a delicious shiver along my spine. It felt good to be away from the chaos of the hospital and to finally be able to relax and reflect on the fact that I had run into Greg Anderson earlier in my shift. It had been an unusually busy evening in the trauma unit, but I still had made time for a decent dinner in the cafeteria and had run into him for the first time since that fateful night in June.

Something about me must have changed, because Greg sat with me and couldn't stop complimenting me on how pretty and relaxed I looked these days. The surprising thing was that it really didn't matter to me what Greg thought of my appearance. In fact, I even asked about his wife and family with sincere interest. I was cured! Greg Anderson was no longer capable of hurting me. I had reclaimed my power.

I took another sip of my mineral water and began mentally downshifting from high-strung, super-responsible nurse, to mellowed out, tranquil, music lover. I thought of one of Joe's commandments for me, the one about enjoying every moment. How right he had been. Never before would I have been aware of what joy there is in not just an event itself, but in the very anticipation of it. Before meeting

Joe, I would have been too impatient to savor the moments building up to hearing the music I loved most, the music that touched me somewhere deep in my soul and made me feel as if the musician who created it must know me very well. I smiled to myself thinking of all the contentment Joe had brought into my life.

Someone bumped my shoulder, jolting me back to the moment. I found myself looking at a black leather jacket, and my gaze followed the silver zipper further up where a curious-looking medal hung from a very muscular neck. Even further, and I saw a roguish five o'clock shadow on an angular face and just a hint of dimples in both corners of a sensitive mouth. His hair was as black as the jacket he wore, and it was kind of wild and unruly in a boyish sort of way.

"I like your smile," he said without any hint of barroom phoniness. Unknowingly, he had said something that healed me of that old self-consciousness about my crooked teeth. In spite of my attempt to eliminate my ego, I blushed and smiled even wider.

"Thanks," I murmured, not knowing what

else to say to this rather magnetic man. Why did I find him so charming? He had only said one sentence to me and already I felt somewhat drawn to him. Was I just desperate? I hadn't thought so. Or was it that in a way, he reminded me of Joe? Yeah, that must be it. The more I studied him, the more I could see the similarities.

"What are you thinking so hard about?" he asked as he took a swig from the bottle in his hand, and I noticed with some surprise that he was drinking the same thing I was, mineral water. Not too long ago, I would have immediately labeled him a health nut, but now I was impressed by a man who was secure enough to walk into a bar and order mineral water. I watched his Adam's apple bob as he swallowed the healthy gulp he'd taken, and I couldn't help but smile.

He looked down at me and returned my smile. "What's so funny," he asked, ready for a good laugh.

"I wasn't laughing at you," I replied, wishing I could come up with some kind of witty remark. Then I heard Joe inside my head reminding me to be myself, to let go of the ego. "I was just thinking of a good friend of mine," I said. "And thinking of him always makes me smile."

"Lucky man," said the tall stranger.

"Oh, no. It's not like that," I hastened to point out, not understanding why it was so important to let this enticing new acquaintance know that I was unattached.

"Does that mean you're here by yourself?" he asked, dark brown eyes dancing and flirting at the same time. I lowered my eyes bashfully. "Don't be coy," he teased.

"Okay," I answered, about to break every one of the rules I'd learned in women's magazines about snaring a man by never letting him see your real self. "I'm here by myself," I stated proudly. "I love Jim MaGuire's music, and nothing in this world would have kept me away tonight."

"Good for you." He grinned. "You have excellent taste. I like his music too. I wonder why he's not that well known."

"The truly great ones never are," I remarked with exaggerated sympathy. Then I began to babble and I couldn't stop myself. "His music does something to me, you know? It turns my heart into melted butter."

"Oooh, I like that," he said with a grin that made me a little weak in the knees. Why was I suddenly so attracted to this complete stranger? I thought I knew better than that. As if on cue, he then asked my name and held out a broad, yet graceful hand. Suddenly I felt like a schoolgirl or a timid little rabbit.

I slipped my hand inside his and said, "I'm Christine," hoping my voice didn't reveal how utterly charmed I was.

"Christine what?" he asked gently, the way a big, kind policeman might speak to a frightened child. He was irresistible.

"Christine Moore," I said, a little more confidently, noticing the sliver of diamond he had pierced through one ear.

"Well, Christine," he replied with a teasing glint in his eye, "I hope I get to see *Moore* of you." With that, he lifted my hand to his soft lips and planted a whisper of a kiss on my fingers.

I was speechless for a moment as he excused himself and disappeared into the crowd before

I even had a chance to ask him his name. Damn, I thought. Why are the cute ones always so elusive?

"He's not elusive," a voice behind me said, "just a little preoccupied."

I knew before turning around that Joe would be standing behind me, hearing my thoughts, as usual. "Preoccupied with what?" I demanded of him. "Aren't I enough to hold a man's attention for more than five minutes?"

Joe shook his head. "You know better than that, Christine. Why do you automatically assume that some shortcoming in *you* is responsible for another's erratic behavior?"

"Good question," I had to admit. "Why *do* I do that?"

"You tell me," Joe challenged. "It's time you stopped relying on me to answer these basic questions for you. Try trusting your own judgment."

There was not even a hint of impatience in his tone, yet I was surprised at Joe's reluctance to just hand me an answer the way he had since I'd met him.

"Well, it's probably just a very bad habit of mine," I said. "I mean, you're right, I *do* know

135

better than to assume there's something wrong with me just because some person I don't even know doesn't seem interested."

"Go on," Joe encouraged. "Why do you do it then?"

"Laziness," I said triumphantly. "I've been too lazy to break a bad habit. It's easier to blame my unhappiness on some imagined shortcoming of mine, rather than realizing that people have all kinds of reasons for not wanting to get involved with each other and that is just the way it is. It is in no way a reflection on me."

"Very good." Joe clapped his hands, my one-man fan club.

"It took a lot of thinking to get to that point," I said, laughing. "No wonder I took the lazy way out for so many years."

"I'll tell you a little secret," Joe said through a smile.

"What?"

"That guy is not only interested in you, he is absolutely *bowled over* by you."

"Yeah, right. Don't tease," I said, pouting. "I suppose that's why he walked away."

"You're hopeless sometimes, Christine." Joe chuckled as he gave my ponytail an affectionate tug. "The guy walked away because he didn't know how to respond to how attracted he is to you."

"Oh, c'mon," I said in utter disbelief. "How do you know that?"

Joe said nothing and just cocked an eyebrow, waiting for the lightbulb to go on in my brain.

"Oh, of course!" I said, not a minute too soon. "You're God, you know everything!"

"I wish you'd quit thinking of me as God," Joe said a bit irritably. "The term is so outdated." He took my glass of mineral water from my hand and took a long, slow swallow. "My work with you is almost done, Christine," he continued, "but I won't feel comfortable until I know you think of me as more of a guide or something. Your perception of 'God' is a bit inaccurate and I've decided to discourage that image." He looked lovingly at me with those magnetic brown eyes and lowered his voice to a hoarse whisper. "I want to be more than that to you, Christine, more than some big guy in the sky who keeps score of all your wrongdoings."

Now it was my turn to laugh. For once, *he* should have known better. "Of course you mean more to me than that," I soothed. Surprisingly, I felt tears of tenderness sting my eyes, but I made no effort to banish them. Joe had taught me well. I reached for his warm, soft hand and held it to my cheek. "You've taught me so much, Joe," I said earnestly. "And I love you so much. And now that I understand that stuff about how you are me and I am you, I can finally relax into being who I really am and love myself for it. That's the most loving gift I've ever known." I knew the tears were shining in my eyes, and it didn't surprise me at all to see tears shining in Joe's eyes as well.

Wordlessly, he wrapped his strong arms around me and kissed the top of my head. "You've been a star student," he murmured, "especially tonight."

"Oh, you mean that stuff about not blaming myself for everything?" I said absently.

"No, I'm talking about the way you ran into your old boyfriend at work—what's his name?"

I broke from his arms and looked up into that beautiful face. "Greg Anderson? Is that who you're talking about?" I asked, amazed that I had already forgotten about my encounter earlier tonight in the hospital cafeteria.

"Yeah, him," Joe said. "Six weeks ago, you

were destroyed by the fact that he married someone else. Tonight you run into him and it doesn't even faze you. It doesn't hurt anymore. That's progress!"

"Yeah, I guess it is," I said, laughing, shocked at such a glaring example of my personal growth.

"Hey, I have something for you," Joe said as he reached into his jacket pocket and retrieved a gift-wrapped box, the kind jewelry usually comes in.

Unable to speak for the wild anticipation and utterly confusing emotions that were running rampant in my poor, overstimulated mind, I clumsily opened the box. It got hard to breathe as I opened the lid and peered inside. There, in the middle of some cotton stuffing, sat a piece of gold in the shape of the tablets that Moses was famous for carrying down the mountain. I read the lengthy inscription on it:

1. Do not build walls, for they are dangerous. Learn to transcend them.
2. Live in the moment, for each one is precious and not to be squandered.
3. Take care of yourself, first and foremost.

4. Drop the ego. Be real. And watch what happens.
5. All things are possible all of the time.
6. Maintain Universal Flow. When someone gives, it is an act of generosity to receive. For in the giving, there is something gained.

"I don't ever remember discussing that last one, Joe," I said, recovering from my chaotic emotions.

"I know," he said. "That's why I included an explanation on it. I got a little behind schedule with you. It's the last one you have to learn and you're going to need a lot of practice on this one. You know, being a nurse and all, you tend to give far more than you allow yourself to receive."

The man knew me like a book. I had always been far more comfortable giving to people, fixing them and rescuing them, rather than allowing anyone to give to me. It had always been far easier to focus on the needs of other people, because if I had ever stopped to examine my own longings, I was afraid there would be no end to them. It was time now to look at my own needs and begin to fulfill them one at a time.

Then a terrible thought struck me. Was this the end? Had this been a farewell gift? I wasn't ready to let go of him. There was still so much I had to learn; still so much I needed from him.

"What we have will never end, Christine," he said tenderly, anticipating my unasked question. "Now you know that I am real and any time you doubt my existence, you have only to look at those little gold tablets to know that all of this really happened."

Oh, no. It was true. He was saying good-bye. Tears started spilling down my face as the realization sunk in. "Please don't go," I begged lamely.

"You have nothing to be concerned about," Joe soothed as he wiped a tear from my face for the last time in this lifetime. "I won't leave you empty-handed. There are so many good things on their way to you, you can't even imagine." He brushed a strand of hair out of my eyes and anchored it behind my ear. "Just promise me you'll always keep an open mind and that you'll never doubt me again or forget about our time together."

I was incredulous. How could he even imagine I would *ever* forget? Just then, the lights blinked off, filling the room with darkness. The sweet strains of Jim MaGuire's saxophone permeated the air as a blue light outlined the silhouette of a man with longish, curly hair playing his horn as though it were a part of him.

I looked up at Joe, desperately wanting to burn his image into my memory, knowing that this would be the last time in my life that I would see him. "Who's next?" I asked, wondering where he would be off to in an effort to complete his list of people on this earth who needed their own personal set of commandments. He knew what I meant and he squeezed my hand.

"See that girl over there?" he said, pointing to a tall blond in a skintight miniskirt. My heart sank.

"Did you have to pick such a . . . a . . . sexy one?" I asked miserably.

Joe laughed at me and I knew why. "We're going to have to do some work on her wardrobe too," he said with a teasing wink. He turned back to me and lifted my chin up with his long forefinger. "Remember," he murmured over the beautiful saxophone music in the background, "I'm never farther away than a whisper." Then he kissed the tip of my nose and sauntered off in the direction of the unsuspecting, lucky girl in the skintight miniskirt.

I watched until he was just a dark and indefinable figure in a dim and crowded room. I leaned forlornly on the bar. Now what? What would life be without Joe? Of course, I knew the answer. Life would be everything Joe said it would be as long as I remembered to live by all he had taught me.

I lifted my head and drank in Jim MaGuire's lovely music, determined to live in the present moment and not to squander any of the joy Joe had taught me to appreciate. And then a funny thing happened.

The silhouette on stage who was pouring his heart out through his saxophone began to look familiar. He *was* familiar. The tall, lanky body, the long, unruly hair, and the silver medal resting on his chest, made it clear who he was. I had been flirting with Jim MaGuire. *Me! The* Jim MaGuire!

I've always despised the kind of women who

faint over rock stars, but suddenly I had a new perspective on their behavior. Not that I was going to faint, but I couldn't wipe the look of total amazement off my face.

Jim MaGuire finished his set of musical masterpieces to a grateful and admiring audience. The crowd was animated and electrified by his performance, but I sat dumbstruck on my barstool, wondering what could possibly happen next. I watched him shake hands with his fans as he made his way through the crowd, heading in my general direction.

It took a lifetime, but finally he was standing in front of me, all flushed and exhilarated from the expression of his music.

"Why didn't you tell me?" I asked, feeling a little foolish that I had raved about his music without knowing who he was. What if I had said something unflattering instead?

"Would it have mattered if you knew who I was?" he asked with a grin. "Besides, it's nice to get an *honest* review," he added before I could answer the question.

"Well, what if I had said I *hated* your music?" I said defensively.

"Not much chance you'd be here if you felt like that," he answered with a victorious look in his eye.

"Well, to answer your question," I said, "no it wouldn't have mattered either way who you were. I've learned to always give honest answers. Life's much easier that way."

He lifted his bottle of mineral water into the air and toasted, "To honesty. How refreshing." He took a gulp of the cool liquid and smiled down at me, causing me to blush. "I really do like your smile," he said sweetly. "Something about you just strikes me as so real. I'm very attracted to you."

That was it! He'd said the magic word. He was *attracted* to me. I had attracted him, not approached him. Isn't that what Joe had tried to tell me that day at lunch? Something about my enlightened and contented soul "attracting" an enlightened man. Now I knew for certain that somehow, some way, Joe was always going to be with me.

"Listen," Jim MaGuire was saying over the din, "you want to go for a quick spin on my motorcycle? I still have twenty minutes before my next set."

This was too perfect, except that now I knew there was no such thing as *too* perfect. Everything was just the way it was supposed to be. Jim MaGuire offered me his hand, and I took it, relaxing and letting him lead the way through the crowd and out into the steamy summer night. I didn't feel like I was relinquishing anything like control or power. It just felt good to allow myself to receive something I never used to allow. I was in control; I always had been. What was different now was that I no longer felt I had to prove it.

I stood aside fastening the helmet Jim handed me as he started the engine. He pulled out of the parking space, and I expertly climbed on behind him. I wrapped my arms around him as our heads jerked backward and we took off into the magical summer night.

Life was such an adventure now. So many things had changed, but mostly *I* had changed, and that had been the catalyst my world had needed. I couldn't think of a more fitting way to ride into my new life than on the back of a Harley with a man who exposed his soul through a saxophone.

We pulled up to a red light, and Jim looked

over his shoulder at me and smiled. I smiled
back and touched the silver chain on the back
of his neck. I pulled the thick sterling silver
medal around to the back and examined it in
the glow of the stoplight. I couldn't quite make
out the image on it, so I leaned closer into him
for a better look. It was Joseph of Nazareth.

And he winked at me.

Author Note

Joan Brady is a freelance writer, a registered nurse, and a former lifeguard. She lives in California.